I0681367

Shadow Out of the Sky

Shadow Out of the Sky

Book One of the Transitional Delusions Series

Brick Marlin

SEVENTH STAR PRESS

Copyright © 2014 by Brick Marlin
All rights reserved. No portion of this book may be copied or transmitted in any form, electronic or otherwise, without express written consent of the publisher or author.

Cover art: Jason C. Conley
Cover art in this book copyright © 2014 Jason C. Conley & Seventh Star Press, LLC.

Interior Illustrations Enggar Adirasa
Interior illustrations © 2014 Tim Holtrop & Seventh Star Press

Editor: Rodney Carlstrom

Published by Seventh Star Press, LLC.

ISBN Number: 978-1-941706-20-6

Seventh Star Press
www.seventhstarpress.com
info@seventhstarpress.com

Publisher's Note:
Shadow Out of the Sky is a work of fiction. All names, characters, and places are the product of the author's imagination, used in fictitious manner. Any resemblances to actual persons, places, locales, events, etc. are purely coincidental.

Printed in the United States of America

First Edition

Acknowledgements

This novel would not have been possible without the huge support from my wife, Lori Marlin, leaving me alone so I could stuff myself in my office and piece together the beginning of this bizarre world entitled Transitional Delusions. I'd like to give praise and thanks to my publisher, Stephen Zimmer (A.K.A. The Almighty Zimm); my editor, Rodney Carlstrom; my illustrators, Jason Conley and Enggar Ajar A; friends I've known for quite some time, Chuck Lewis, Kathy Copas, Calvin Lewis, Tim, Shawna, Brendon, Zack Lewis; and lastly, two great authors, awesome friends, who have given me the help and support to move forward in this literary masquerade, Gary A. Braunbeck and Lucy Snyder.

Chapter 1

"Momma?" a voice cut through the dark.

"Charlie?" Her daughter's voice startled her. When she looked, a small shadow stood in the doorway. "Are you okay?"

"Yeah. I had a bad dream." The shadow shifted to the left, clutching something in.

"Well, honey, it's okay now." Karen slid her legs over, hung them off the bed. "Come here."

Charlie walked to her mom and sat beside her. Karen slipped an arm around her daughter.

"Is Bear-Bear in your arms?"

"Yeah. He keeps me safe."

"Sure he does." Karen yawned, using her palm to cover her mouth. She closed her eyes for a second then opened them. "He always has, hasn't he, honey?"

"Yeah."

The only light in the room came from the moon. Outside the wind blew against the window pane.

"Whew…the wind's whipping out there," Karen said.

"I know," Charlie replied. "Momma?"

"Yes?" Karen could smell the watermelon scent of the shampoo still in Charlie's hair from her bath the night before.

"Do you miss daddy?"

"Aw, honey, you know I do. You miss him, too. Don't you?"

"Yeah. I miss him bunches and bunches."

"So do I Charlie. But I'm pretty sure God is taking good care of him."

"You do?" Charlie said, surprised, such as when a child discovers something new.

Karen smiled. She wished she could see her daughter's face better. "Yes, I do very much."

"You still love him, don't you?"

"Why sure, why wouldn't I?" *What an odd question, but aren't children's questions weird at times?*

"Do you think you will ever get to meet him, Mommy?"

"Well… I'm sure I will." An uneasy feeling touched Karen's spine and she pulled away from her. The thought of death grabbing her hand and leaving her daughter behind did not give her a bit of delight. Who would raise Charlie if she died? If Annie did, Karen would probably roll over in her grave because her sister didn't act very responsible. She had no kids. Not even a job. She mooched off the government playing the disability card.

Karen shuddered.

"It'll probably be when God calls me to come home," Karen said, trying to give the best answer she could. "But, Charlie, I don't think it'll be for a very, very long while. God wants to make sure you're okay and you grow up to be a bigger girl than you are right now." She paused. "Now Charlie." She sighed. "Why would you ask, anyway?"

"Because Bear-Bear wanted to know. He asked *me* to ask *you*."

"Oh. Bear-Bear asked, huh?" Karen smiled again.

"Yeah. He wanted to know." A sliver of the moon's color outlined a quarter of Charlie's face as she leaned forward, showing her right eye, a pitch black pupil.

Karen did not catch sight of it.

"Well, Bear-Bear," she said to the toy, "I'm going to be fine. Don't worry."

Charlie's face materialized back into the dark and the temperature dropped twenty degrees.

"Karen reached over and wrapped herself in a loose blanket. It lay at the foot of the bed. "There must be a draft coming through the window."

Charlie became oddly silent as the wind rattled the window pane.

"Charlie? You okay? Are you cold?"

"A little."

"Here," Karen held the blanket up next to her, inviting her daughter to slip inside. "Get warm."

Karen didn't adjust to Charlie's ice cold skin right away when her hand fell on the small arm. When she had placed her arm around Charlie before, it only hung off her shoulders. However, Karen winced from the pain shortly after Charlie pressed up against her, the sharp point slicing through her flesh.

She didn't quite comprehend the shadow lurking in the corner, watching closely, intent of absorbing the horror.

Karen cried out, allowing the blood fill her throat, leak through her lips. Her vision started to fade, but captured the family photograph on the night stand. Her arms around Charlie, her husband Steven holding them both in a hug. Steven died a few years prior by slipping off the dock at his job, his body never found in the currents of the fast-moving river.

In the glow of the moonlight the point slid out, returned, each time with more force.

***

Bobby stepped in out of the cold and sat his briefcase down in the hallway. The lights were off. Dana always had a few lights blazing in the house—more than a few, too—at this time of night.

At first, he feared something wrong. But he thought it to be a simple power outage.

"Dana? You upstairs?" he said.

In the living room he heard their cat meow.

"Hey, Sparks. You okay?"

Another meow returned, as if in reply.

Bobby started up the steps. His boy stood at the top. "You okay, son? Where's your mom?"

"She's in the bedroom, Daddy."

"Oh. Why are all of the lights out, Matthew?"

"Mommy said the wind blew the power out."

"Figures…" He shook his head. He reached into his jacket and pulled out his cell phone. The blue glow of the screen shoved a small patch of the dark away. He used his internet app to find the utility company's website and number and dialed.

"Dad?"

"Yeah, son?" His eyes flicked upward.

"Are you coming up?"

"In a minute… Hello? Yes, this is Bobby Vincent out here on Johnstown Road. I wondered if there was a power outage. There is? Okay… well, thanks. How long before it's fixed? Okay, thanks. Bye."

"Daddy?"

Bobby looked up at his son again. "Yeah. Hang on, Matthew, I'm coming." He slid the phone back into his jacket.

"I think mommy's hurt, Daddy."

"Hurt?" His stomach knotted up.

"I think she fell or something."

Bobby hurried up the steps, brushing past his son, slipped into the bedroom, a landscape with moonlight shrouded over the walls and bed where Dana lay on her side covered in a white sheet.

"Dana? You okay, Hon?"

She didn't respond, nor did she move.

"Dana?" Bobby sat next to where she lay and placed a hand on her shoulder. "You okay? Are you hurt?"

Dana remained silent. When Bobby turned her over, the moonlight showed the damage: meaty, open flesh. The second before he screamed something cut into his spine, twisted, turned, until the bones of the vertebrae popped loose, detaching under his flesh.

Little Matthew, their first child, their loving son who would never harm a soul, the one who loved to be read to before bed and still wanted the night light on, stood behind his father. He clutched the long knife from the one drawer in the kitchen accessible to be reached inside with small, fragile hands.

The moonlight highlighted the once protruding belly of Dana and what lay dead beside her corpse, cut free of her flesh.

Chapter 2

Dean sat in the recliner and glanced at the digital clock on the cable box while rolling his eyes back to the old sc-fi flick on the television. Digging these movies since he was a kid, he watched huge mutant roaches attack a human colony. The defense of the colony failed miserably, beaten back. Some torn apart or eaten by the large bugs.

His cell phone rang.

"Hey there handsome," the voice on the other end spoke.

"Hey there." A grin spread under Dean's nose.

"I wanted to see what the man of the house has been doing while his wife is away tonight. Lonely? Need some company?"

"Well, I don't know...maybe."

"Maybe?"

"Sure, I guess so. C'mon over. She doesn't get home until late. We can go upstairs, run a bath, and if we're not too worn out from playing in the tub, we can finish up by sliding into bed. Afterwards I'd have to clean up the evidence. You know how Rachael keeps the house clean. She's overly compulsive when it comes to it. Why, the other day she got all over me because I placed a fork in the wrong spot, on top of the spoons in the drawer. Then, there was that time—"

"Dean."

"Yes."

"You're not being very funny."

"I thought so."

Rachael chuckled on the other end of the line. Dean loved to hear her do it. He could picture her face all lit up. "Dean, you're something else, you know it?"

"Sure I do. I married you, didn't I? Have to be something, or another. Or crazy."

"Crazy in love is what you are, Mr. Clemins." Rachael knew Dean loved her. She loved him more than anything in the world. Lately they were trying to have a baby.

One of her friends, a coworker at County General hospital, had told her a story about trying to have a baby. The couple had worked at it so much, the sex became more of a job than a pleasure. They almost decided on adoption, but they weren't sure. They also weren't so sure if they wanted to take the *in vitro* fertilization road and have ten children, versus, only the two they were setting out to have.

Rachael's friend did finally end up pregnant, though, after two years of trying.

So, as the days progressed, Rachael and Dean were content with the idea on conceiving a child. Rachael did not want it to be a chore. She wanted to keep it interesting, romantic, and spontaneous. Let nature take its course. Rachael prayed every night and hoped God would show them the path.

Maybe they could eventually move out of their small house, buy some land, and build a bigger house to accommodate the two children they were hoping to have.

Yep, their dream.

"Yeah. I'm crazy for you," Dean said. "Ya got me there."

"Thought so. Leave any food for me?"

"A spoonful."

"Once again, Dean, the travelin' comedian."

"There's plenty, Rachel. Don't worry."

"Good. Listen, I'll be getting off in an hour, unless we get any busier here in the ER, okay?"

"Getting off, you say?"

"Dean, you have a dirty mind. Anyone ever tell you that?"

"Somewhere along the line, yes."

"Well, look, I'll see you soon. Love you."

"Love you." Dean hit the off button on the cell phone and reclined back in the chair to watch three humans slaughter a huge roach with their laser beams. Its guts spilled all over them, turning into maggots, scurrying and began burrowing into their flesh.

Dean winced.

Chapter 3

Shro, short for Schroeder, sat on the barstool at Scooter's kicking back his fifth shot of whiskey. He burped. Only damn thing good in life, he thought, is drinking. His day at work, a stinking sewer hole they called Hile's Lumberyard where he worked in receiving, unloading trucks all day long, had been busy. He had seniority over most of the guys, especially the young ones who worked there while they went to the uppity college ten miles away. Expensive, affluent, nose in the air, my crap don't stink kind of school. Supposedly one of the better schools in the country. Big deal. His education came from Hampshire High back in the late eighties. Hell, he had ended up mighty fine without going to college.

Hell, he had a wife, a stepson, a good job, a house on a street backed up against the woods, an old truck and a 1970 Plymouth Barracuda sitting in the garage.

He loved the car dearly.

Even if it didn't have an engine. Or a hood. Or four inflated tires. Or a front windshield. It did have, though, the original radio. Shro could still tune it in on 780 a.m. and hear the oldies: Buddy Holly, Fats Domino, Chuck Berry, Bill Haley and the Comets, etc. The list went on and on.

Yeah, a favorite of his on Saturday evenings, sitting in the decrepit husk of the Barracuda, have a beer in one hand with the rest of the six pack in the backseat. He'd lean back, turn on 780, and imagine driving the Plymouth out on the open road. He envisioned the world whipping by, girls in their mini-skirts shouting and squealing, blowing wet kisses at him, unbuttoning their tops to reveal their big 'ol —

"Shro?"

The dreamer's hazel eyes blinked. Scooter, the proprietor and bartender, appeared in front of him. "Want another?" Scooter held up the half-empty whiskey bottle.

"Mmmm...Don't know. Think I'll get a ticket for driving drunk?" Shro smirked.

Scooter smiled, showing two missing teeth on the bottom row. "You very well might, buddy, if Johnny Law catches you out there. You know Gabe is patrolling the streets tonight."

"He couldn't patrol his way out of his cruiser," Shro said, slurring a bit. "He's probably gettin' some from Betty, his girl. He ain't gonna be around nowhere."

Scooter chuckled. "Shro, you're one of a kind, man. Always have been. Ever since school." He walked over and poured another golden shot into the tiny glass.

Shro kicked it back and it slid down his throat. "I know, Scoot. We go back a ways. Me 'n' you. Remember when we got Daryl Flipo...Flipposwit...Er, Flipposhot...Flippo—"

"Flipposwith. Daryl Flipposwith. Yeah, I remember. You know he's some kind of big writer now?"

"Writer?" Shro snorted.

"Seriously, Shro, seen it in the newspaper the other day. Won some kind of award for one of his novels."

Smiling, Shro said, "The only thing he won was a stuck ass when we smeared super glue on all the seats in the boy's bathroom. Remember? We had to stand there like guards and turn away a bunch of kids until we saw Flipshot."

"Flipposwith."

"Whatever!" Shro waved his hand through the air. "They had to call the fire department and," he chuckled, "the ambulance to get the chump unstuck!"

"Wasn't his father an EMT? He showed up, didn't he?"

"Yeah! What a gay job, Scoot! You shoulda seen his eyes when he saw Flippo!" Shro could barely contain himself, now laughing, lost his balance and fell off the barstool.

"Whoa!" Scooter said. "You okay, man?" A chuckle slipped out of his lips.

There were six others in the bar, including Patty, the waitress. Scooter's main squeeze. Everyone stopped and watched Shro make an ass of himself. They all laughed.

Shro always thought luck favored Scooter, attracting younger women such as Patty. He snuck a peek at Patty. Her bosom rose and fell in the tight halter top she wore as she laughed.

What he wouldn't give for a night with her. Big bosom. Big hips. Long legs. Luscious lips...then there was Wendy, his own wife. Best not to think of Patty, Shro, he scolded himself. But, can't a man window shop and fantasize?

"Here," Scooter poured another shot in his glass, "drink this. It's on the house. Ain't never seen nothin' more funnier, Shro." He smiled.

Shro slid his large butt on the stool, chuckled when he brought the glass to his lips, and kicked it back. "It was funny!"

"So, how's the wife and kid?"

"Wendy? She's the same. Can't cook or clean the house right. Feel I need to put yellow caution tape all the way around the house."

"You don't help her with housework?"

Shro's expression dropped and his eyes glared at Scooter. "Housework? I don't do it. You?"

"Well, yeah, sure. I help Patty with the laundry and cooking and cleanin'."

"Scooter, you whipped or something?"

Scooter winced. "Whipped? Me? Hells no! But I do my part to help Patty. She's a good woman. So is Wendy."

"See," Shro's sniffed, "I'm the man of the house and I bring the money home."

Scooter knew Shro loved to boast, being someone he was not. The guy was a goofball. Why Wendy put up with his crap, Scooter never knew. On the flipside, the guy contributed well to the bar's register. "Wendy brings home money, too, right? She works out at the truck stop by the highway."

"Yup. Doesn't make much, though." Shro frowned. "Tryin' to say she makes more than me?" Shro's defensive side showed up.

Patrons at a nearby table who had been laughing, stopped to look at Shro.

"Shro, calm down. I'm only sayin'," Scooter held up his hands. "we've known each other a long time, right?"

Shro nodded.

"I'm not trying to make trouble with you. It may be a good thing if you help her out doin' house chores, since she does work, too."

"Scooter, it's not the way *I* was brought up. My father didn't have to cook and clean. He worked ten hours a day and barely brought enough money home to put a roof over our head."

Scooter knew of Shro's father. Lazy, undercutting work, he ripped both his customers and employees off. His construction company had so many complaints it was finally shut down by the Better Business Bureau and fines were issued.

Scooter didn't mention this. One time when Shro drank way too much he became hostile. The cops had to be called and Shro spent a night in jail. Shro didn't speak to Scooter for two weeks after, but eventually came crawling back to the bar, apologizing for his actions. Scooter took the guy back. Hell, he considered Shro a friend. He tried to keep the peace with him. In a way, though, he hated himself as a bully, alongside Shro. Thank goodness it was in the past.

At least Shro had grown up a bit, though not by much, since he and Shro had left high school. If Shro had hooked up with Wendy back then, she would have kicked him to the curb the first time he tried to be a smartass with her. Wendy didn't put up with a lot of crap. Scooter thought, too, Shro loved boasting his "macho self" outside the house. He knew damn well he would never do it around Wendy.

"Shro," Scooter said, "your woman works, too. You should help her around the house."

Shro grumbled, the alcohol took its course on him tonight. "Not happening. I work longer hours than she does. I shouldn't have to do anything but come home, grab a beer, turn on the TV and wait for my dinner."

Scooter wanted to roll his eyes.

"Do you know that boy of hers thinks he's gonna be an artist or somethin'? I think he said he wanted to be a cartoonist and draw superheroes. He stays in his room and draws a lot. Needs to be out there in the garage, gettin' his hands dirty, while workin' on the 'Cuda."

"Sounds like the boy has high hopes. Maybe it'll find him a ticket out of this country town and he'll make somethin' of himself," Scooter said. "Be good for him."

"No it isn't!" Shro snapped. "Ain't nobody in this little town ever amounted to anything."

"Uh, Flipposwith did," Scooter said cautiously.

"Oh. Well. He don't count. He wasn't anyone to begin with! Shoot!" He chuckled. "Give me a beer, will ya? I need to get on the road soon. Get home. We're gonna reheat leftovers from last night."

"Um, I don't know, Shro. Think you've had enough tonight. Why don't I make you some coffee, huh?"

"Don't want no coffee," Shro said. "Give me a beer, Scooter. I'll be fine. a-okay, man!"

Scooter poured Scooter a beer. He was going to drive the guy home. No way was Shro leaving on his own.

Wendy would have both of their heads on a silver platter.

Chapter 4

Barry Freckles sank his overweight body into his recliner and drank while the world revolved around him. The TV glowed in the darkness; an old rerun of *The Outer Limits* played. Barry had grown up watching the show. At times, it crept him the hell out!

As a boy he would race down to the matinee on First and Oak and pay fifty cents to watch movies involving creatures living in faraway galaxies, along with other monsters lurking in the darkness, feasting on blood and flesh.

Only if allowed by his momma. Only if he did what she instructed him to do before he left the house.

Love your momma, Barry, your mama needs attention...

Her tender words sat in his brain and simmered. His childhood history had been complex, different, morbid. His mother worked at one of the factories in Woodbury barely making enough money for the two to survive. Times were hard after his father's death, but she stretched her paycheck the best she could, affording a roof over their heads and food in their bellies.

Barry's father had never been Father of the Year. The man would come home from work, drunk after stopping over at the bar with the guys, and shout and beat on his mother. He never lifted a finger to Barry, merely ignored the child. The guy hated kids. More than once he claimed bringing one into the world had been the worst thing in life he helped do.

So as Barry's father's displeasure of Barry's mom conceiving another mouth to feed, he repeatedly took out his hate on Barry's mom two to three times a week. Hiding the bruises with makeup, Barry's mom would continue to go to work. She so wished to take Barry and leave. Travel far away from her husband. She wanted a better life for herself and her son.

But, she didn't. Afraid the man would hunt them both down and beat or kill them both, she escaped the abusive venue by drinking and taking prescription meds. She could have as many multicolored pills as she wanted too, as long as she did a little something special for the old perverted doctor at the clinic while in his office, the door shut.

Barry's father died driving home drunk one night and slamming into an oak tree doing ninety miles an hour. The papers said his head had been severed, flung through the window, and lodged into a tree.

Memories of those words haunted Barry. He tried to push them away, tipping the whiskey bottle back, letting the liquid burn his throat. He didn't want to return to the past. He didn't want to keep the door open so the light would slip out, grab him, pull him in and continuously hear the voice raked down his spine: "Come here, Barry, momma needs lovin' tonight. You ain't got no daddy no more. He killed his awful self." She would laugh. The drugs the doc gave her, Barry thought melted her brain. She eventually became different and her moods changed frequently.

Barry had to admit, though, she loved her child dearly.

Even between the sheets.

Love your momma, Barry, love her so special...

After taking an early retirement, as the years went by, momma eventually passed away during the night in her sleep with Barry by her side, her cold arm draped over his naked chest, pressing her hard nipples into his back. Barry had to use money from the small buyout she received from the factory, to bury her. He inherited the house, the memories, and the smell of his mother — some kind of left over residue.

Later, he took a job working down at the garage, changing oil and fixing tires to make ends meet. He had to make a living somehow, because the funeral home took most of his mother's retirement, charging a steep price to bury her.

His nightmares, though, were an entirely different matter. They slipped into his brain and squirmed around. He didn't want them. Very sorry for what he had done, the horrors lurked. May God have mercy on his soul, he would tell himself over and over, trying to convince himself.

Sometimes it sounded convincing, even coming through his lips.

He didn't want to kill the boys. He only wanted to play with him.

He didn't want to kill the sweet little girls. They were so pretty, so soft, so loveable. Barry needed a playmate living alone.

Barry stood up, staggered, dropped the bottle—lucky it had been empty—and it rolled over by the lit fireplace. He could hear cars pass by back and forth in front of his house. He wondered if there would come a day he would have a visit from the Law.

Inevitable. Yes. They would, one day, come. They would find out what he did. His past would come back to haunt him.

He could still feel the flesh under his fingers; so pale, so soft, so young...

Through the back window in the kitchen he could see the woods. So dark and secluded; especially, for the small bodies who were buried deep within the soil. Barry made sure they were hidden away, far from his back porch. Could he still remember how many steps it took to reach the graves? Sure. He'd have to dig into his memories, though. Used to, he had it down pat.

Love your momma, Barry, love her tonight. Make her feel alive again. Barry, my only son...

"Get outta my head!" Barry screamed and knocked over a kitchen chair and it fell down on the linoleum floor. "Get outta my head, momma," he mumbled, tears filling his eyes. "Get outta...my head..."

Crawling in front of the counter, he grabbed hold the edge of the sink, pulled himself upright. Grabbing another full bottle of booze from the cabinet, he slid back down to the floor, twisted off the cap, and drank.

Chapter 5

The last thing Rachael had to deal with at work had been a guy who complained of terrible stomach pain and in dying need of medication to sooth it. After the X-rays came back showing negative results and the urine test came back positive for drugs, the doctor kindly told the gentleman the guy needed to stop the use of drug abuse. Instead of calling the cops, he tried to be nice. Plus, he didn't want to stay over longer than he had to because he had already worked fifteen hours straight. Releasing the patient from the ER, he warned the addict he needed to stop using drugs because it would eventually catch up and kill him.

The guy argued, raising his voice, hollering at the staff and doctors, saying they were worthless and he threatened to file a complaint on their "malpractice."

Unfortunately, the police had to be called anyway and the guy escorted out in cuffs, shouting at the top of his lungs. Rachael wondered if the guy would ever smarten up. Probably not.

Glad to get out of there, it had been a madhouse with two people hurt seriously in a hit-and-run, a small boy who had pneumonia, four cases of the stomach flu, and a young Peeping Tom who broke his arm climbing a tree.

Rachael took the back roads instead of the main highway to get back to Hampshire because of heavy traffic. Construction of the highway had started this week and had pissed off more than a few morning motorists. According to the *Hampshire Herald*, one of the construction guys had a run in with one guy in a Lexus who spit on him. The worker threw a small hammer at the car's window and smashed it. A fist fight between the two had broken out, leaving the police to be called to break it up.

Rachael wanted to get home and relax with Dean. Maybe she could get him to rub her feet and perhaps give her a bath. She had been in a sexual mood ever since she had spoken with Dean earlier.

She truly wanted to keep it romantic and spontaneous, instead of working hard at it and losing the interest in sex. She hoped Dean wouldn't think of her fat, unattractive, or less sexy after being pregnant.

Excited, ready to be a mother, Rachael knew she shouldn't rush it. Let God choose the path.

A sign ahead read: HAMPSHIRE 8 MILES

Not far now, she thought. Stacy's Stop should be close by on the right-hand side of the road all lit up. She wondered if she should fill up the Honda or not, the needle being a tick below the half mark.

She decided to skip it and when she passed Stacy's she was kind of glad she hadn't. Not a single gas pump open.

Closer to Hampshire, traffic lightened, only passing a few cars or a truck. Three miles to go she rounded a curve and her headlights spotted movement slipping into the woods.

Rachael first thought of deer, and slowed down a bit, taking notice to the posted yellow and black diamond-shaped warning signs. Usually, a hot spot for Dean's buddy to hunt venison, she hated the thought of an arrow sticking out of a deer or the insides of its meaty neck exposed from a gunshot. It gave her a small shudder to even think of killing such a beautiful animal – much less taking a bite of venison. Dean loved it; but she wouldn't dare try it.

The road curved gently, vacant of vehicles while the full moon left its silver color on the pavement.

Then Rachael spotted a small, clothed figure on the side of the road.

The Honda's headlights illuminated the object, long enough for Rachael to notice it human; not a deer, or some other animal. She passed it, braked, pulled to the shoulder and slipped out.

The thoughts of it being a child pumped through her blood.

Please don't let it be, please don't let it be!

She hoped her vision gave false readings.

But, her thoughts were true.

Crossing to the other side she stood over a young boy who lay flat on his stomach with his face turned toward the woods.

Her stomach knotted up. "Hello? Are you okay?" she asked, bent down. Rachael didn't receive a response. Her training as a nurse told her to not touch someone until she called the EMT's. In this case, she probably needed to call the police first. "Hello? Can you hear me?" she tried again.

The small body didn't move or twitch.

Rachael decided to place her hand on the boy's neck, feeling for a pulse. Dead. "Jesus," she whispered. Now she figured she screwed up because when she got a hold of the cops, they'd question her to why her finger prints were on the corpse. No. She didn't screw up. She was a nurse. Nurses help others.

She couldn't imagine someone doing harm to a child.

So Rachael stood back up, took out her cell phone and punched in 911. A woman's voice said it could not be completed when dialed and to please try your call again. She punched in the same numbers and received no recorded voice, only silence.

She looked at her phone and it said "No Service" over the top of a picture of Dean's smiling face.

"Crap!" she said.

She walked out in the middle of the road, trying to see if she could get a signal on the phone, and came up empty-handed. She looked to the left, to the right, hoping to see a car or truck pass by so she could flag them down.

"Great!" Frustration set in until the emotion changed to horror. She gasped.

The small body had vanished.

Chapter 6

Half an hour to go and Dean knew Rachael would be home soon.

Dean flipped the station after the movie took a turn for the stupid. Only two humans remained and eventually befriended the dreaded roaches and forgave the creatures for slaughtering their family and friends. The humans figured after living on the planet for a month, they had been the invaders who had invaded the creature's habitat. They even had a large dinner together.

Before Dean's finger hit the button to change the channel one of the smaller roaches, six feet tall, opened the lid to a large pot revealing a man's head soaking in a soup.

The next station showed a documentary of villages and towns vanishing without a trace. It even touched base on the Bermuda Triangle and told of ships and planes, never to been seen again.

A little later Dean's cell phone rang, waking him up from a doze. He answered it, only hearing three of his mother's words before silence came. He pulled it away from his ear and saw it didn't have a signal.

Strange... Must be the phone towers having problems.

He laid the phone down and waited. Once he saw it did retrieve a signal, he would try to call his mother back. They lived six hundred miles away, down south.

He glanced at the clock. Rachael should have been home by now, unless she worked over. He thought of calling her, but she may be busy.

The show on TV had changed to a documentary: The mob in the early seventies. An Italian man in his sixties in an expensive three-piece suit sat spoke with a reporter about the hit men they had used who were not Italian. Especially the zips.

Dean's stomach rumbled. He figured it might be wise to dip out some food from the Crockpot and eat a little. He hated to, but he didn't know if he could wait.

After spooning out a small portion onto a plate, he sat back down, took a bite, and picked up the cell phone.

Still no service.

Chapter 7

Scooter pleaded with Shro not to drive drunk and, at first, Shro shook him off. He told him he would be perfectly fine as he stumbled outside in the cool air.

"The hell with the Law! The hell with Gabe!" he told Scooter. They could all kiss his ass!

"Shro, c'mon, man!" Scooter tried to give it another shot. "Don't get stupid and wind up losing your license and taken downtown and placed in the drunk tank."

Shro turned and looked at him, his long hair hung in front of his eyes, "Scooter. I love ya man, but I know what I'm doin'. Drove like this before and was never caught."

"Shro, man..." Scooter shook his head back and forth.

"I'll be...I'll be f...I'll be fi...uh, I'll be okay, Scoot," Shro slurred as his vision gave him a revolving world. "I only have to drive three...three miles up the road." Shro tried to hold up three fingers, failing miserably.

Scooter sighed. "All right, Shro. Fine!" He held up his hands. "Don't call me to bail you out if you get thrown in the drunk tank."

"Won't need to call ya, c—cause I'm, I'm not g—gonna be in it!" Shro's lips stretched back in a grin and his wobbly legs carried him to his old truck where he opened the door — which took a few tries — and crawled inside.

"Uh... Shro?" Scooter walked over.

"Yeah." Shro dug his keys out of his pocket and searched for the slot to slide his key into the ignition.

"You're in the passenger seat."

"Wha—what?" His eyes were wide. "Oh, I knew that! Shoot! Checkin' to see if the glove box door worked. See?" His fingers fumbled for the button, finally finding it, and it popped open spilling out napkins and a pair of sunglasses. "Th—there."

He grinned again, proud of himself.

"Hang tight, all right? I'll be right back."

"Wh—where you goin', Scoot?"

"Hang on!" The proprietor ran back inside, gone less than three minutes when he came back with his coat on. "I'm driving you home! Don't tell me no! Patty's gonna come and get me."

"Scooter! I tole you I's f—fine. Look, I'll slide over behind the wheel so a—"

"Oh no you're not!" Scooter hurried over to the driver's side and slipped in before Shro could move into the spot.

"If you're driving me home, and P—Patty's comin' to get you, who's manash...manish...Manashing." He paused, swallowed. "Uh, who's tendin' the bar?"

"No one is. We're closin' up for the night. It's starting to get late anyways and we haven't been busy. You know this town has a curfew."

"Oh. Yeah. Th—thass right."

The old truck's ignition sparked and after a sputter or two, roared to life with smoke billowing out of the pipes.

"Shro, no offense, but the inside of this truck smells, man. Needs some deodorizer or somethin'"

"Ain't nofin' wrong with the odor in here!"

"You can't tell 'cause you're used to it. Probably too drunk to notice it too."

Shro paused, let the thought sink in. "Oh. Guess so."

Scooter drove the truck down the road and hung a left into the town square. Shops sat side by side, some closed up for the evening, some vacant and in need of new owners, with darkness lurking behind the windows. In the middle sat a wooden gazebo on a green lawn. During the summer and fall the town of Hampshire held various festivities. Such as the candy apple eating contest in May, a bluegrass band playing in the gazebo every Saturday during the month of July, a Halloween party for the kids in October. They also held a small fair which called Hampshire Days in September where people would set up booths selling anything from pet insurance to jewelry to food and beer to clothing to ceramic figurines.

"Hey, Shro, look over there," Scooter said, pointing out of his window. "Remember when we were kids and stuck worms in those trays of candy apples when they were gettin' ready to have an apple eatin' contest?"

"Um, yeah." His head wobbled. "I th—think...I think so." Shro's eyes had been closed. Now they were open slits.

"Man, were those people pissed off when they saw worms crawlin' all over the fruit! Only one guy started eating before he found out he had eaten a worm."

"Um. Yeah, think I remember, Scoot."

Scooter gazed at him. "I should have made you drink some coffee before we left. I should have stopped from givin' you anymore booze, early on."

"Aw, Scoot, you know I'll be fine."

"I know you can handle your liquor pretty well — or used to, when you were younger —but, in case you haven't noticed, you've aged since then, buddy."

"Uh? Aw, hell, I'm fine." Shro watched the world through the windshield shimmy and shake. His stomach suddenly became sour.

They drove out of downtown, passing Hampshire High. Shro's

truck dipped down a hill, came back up, and right before they turned onto the road winding back to Shro's place, the passenger rolled down the window and hung his head out and spewed.

"Ugh! That's nasty, Shro! Maybe you need to stop drinking so much."

Shro turned his face toward Scooter, puked dribbling down his chin, and said, "M—Man, and you kept feeding flame to the wood."

"You mean wood to the flame."

"Thass what I said, Scooter."

"No you didn't. You sa—"

"I knows what I said!"

Scooter sighed, shook his head. "Okay, Shro. You win."

"Win?"

Scooter opened his mouth to explain, thought better of it, and said, "Nothin', man."

"What? What are you sayin'?"

"Nothing, Don't worry about it."

"Oh. Okay."

"Roll up the window, Shro, it's cold outside!"

They road in silence, passing a few houses without any lights glowing behind the windows, until they pulled up in front of Shro's house and noticed it, too, held no lights blazing, outside, or in.

"Huh," Scooter said, shifting the transmission into park, "strange." He glanced behind him. "Ain't no lights on anywhere, Shro. Not in your place or anyone else's."

"Wh—What?" Shro's stomach felt better. He rose up and his eyes found his garage with the Mack truck grill nailed over the door, looking for the light he had thought of installing long ago, and then remembered he hadn't yet. He saw the porch light, like Scooter mentioned, was off. "Well, crap! What the hell? Wendy musta forgot to leave the lights on."

"Shro, don't you have a sitter for your boy? Wendy's workin' tonight, right?"

"Yeah. Wendy should be workin'." Shro saw the sitter's small car parked in the driveway. "Well, yeah. The sitter's car is right there." He pointed.

"Oh." Scooter saw it.

"What time is it?"

"Ten."

"Wendy won't be home until twelve. Carolyn is the girl sittin' for us."

"Earl's daughter?"

"Yeah."

"She's a good girl, Shro. Heard from her father —you know he comes in on the weekends with his wife for a drink — that next year she's supposed to go to college."

"At the uppity school?"

"Yeah, think so."

"Oh."

"Look, let me check it out and then you can follow me in. All right? If something's wrong in there, you aren't in any shape or form to do anything."

"You sayin' there might be a burglar in my home?"

"I don't know, man. But I need to find out why there ain't no lights on. Must be a power outage. Your sitter should still be awake." Scooter slipped out of the truck, with the door hinge creaking from its desperate need of oil.

"Scooter, I'm c—comin' with you. It's *my* house!" He placed three fingers on the door latch and pulled.

Scooter slid out of the truck and walked around and held his hand on the door. "No, man. Listen to me!" he cursed through the window. "There may be someone in there and I told you you aren't in any shape or form to go in. Much less having to try and fight them. I'll take care of it."

"Scooter, there's never been any burglars and such around these parts. Everything's probably A. Oh. Kay."

"There's a first for everything, Shro. Stay here, wouldya?"

Shro's fingers fell from the latch and he sighed. "Okay, man. Go check it out. Yell if you need me."

"All right. I will." Scooter turned and walked toward the dark house.

Chapter 8

Wendy worked at Sam's, a truck stop located five miles out near the highway. Fuel stations were out front with the diner behind them. Half of the brick building held a diner; the other half held a convenience store. And right where you enter through the diner's doors they had pamphlets on a rack informing folks of Hampshire's festivities during the year, Woodbury's apple festival, and the spelunking in the town of Fishers Way. Below, on the same rack, were the *Hampshire Herald* and the *Woodbury Times*. Both local newspapers looked thin, as if they were only five pages in length.

A few cars and trucks were filling up at the pumps. People lingered and shopped inside the gift shop, dragging a couple of sleepy children in tow who staggered around.

"Order up for table twelve." Older than the other cooks, young kids making extra cash to pay for their dorm rooms the following year, Gerald played the manager role.

He knew what kids did. He had been one of them long ago. And, sometimes, he would eavesdrop and hear the two converse, 'sleeping with so and so or feeling so and so up'.

Kinda excited the old guy.

"Order up for table twelve," he said again, this time more of a shout.

"I'm coming, I'm coming, Gerald," Wendy said, maneuvering through the opening of the long counter where only two men sat, drinking their coffee. "I was tryin' to clean a table so a customer could have a sit. She didn't want any other table; she chose a particular one."

Gerald smiled. "I know which one I'd want if I came in here."

Wendy frowned.

"I wouldn't want no table. I'd want a pretty little red-headed waitress named, uh...Wendy."

"Cram it, Gerald! You startin' that again? After I told you to lay off?"

"Can't a man make a pleasant comment for a beautiful young lady?"

"Sure. Long as he isn't thinking of how to get her in bed or a quickie in the storage room."

"Aw, now! Come on, Wendy! I didn't mean nothin' by it the other day."

"Like I said to you then, and I'm gonna say it now: keep your hands to yourself! You're lucky Robby isn't here!"

"The owner is hardly here, honey. You know that. I'm the one runnin' the show, most nights." Gerald smiled. His fat, stubbly, face stretched into a grin showing his missing front tooth. His long greasy hair, tied up in a ponytail, neighbored the clear spot directly on top of his head.

"You're pushin' it, Gerald. You want me to walk out of here? I'm the only waitress on duty 'cause little miss-priss- Laura didn't show up for work tonight."

"Wendy, I know you need the money. Your boy's birthday's comin' up soon, right? I heard you tellin' Laura the other night." He sniffed, wiped his nose with the back of his hand. "I know you won't walk out, will ya?"

Wendy couldn't really say she would. God knows she wanted to tell Gerald to stick this whole grease bucket up his ass, but she knew she couldn't. Together, she and Shro's income barely paid the bills.

"Table twelve's food is gettin' cold," Gerald prodded, without losing the grin. "Better get along and serve it to 'em."

Wendy stood for a few seconds longer, grabbed the two plates — one with a cheeseburger and fries, one with a plain hamburger and fries — while Gerald's fingers held onto them, slid over, and lightly touched Wendy's.

She glared at him.

Work around Hampshire had been on the downslide lately, such as trying to find a diamond in the pig slop out on Daryl Sims' farm. An endeavor only pushing down the hopes of low-class folks looking for a decent job with decent pay in an old country town. Shro was one of the lucky ones to have a job working at the lumberyard making somewhat of a decent paycheck.

Wendy's check paid half the bills and Shro's paid the other half, keeping a roof over their heads. She knew Shro spent a little down at Scooter's; sometimes, more than he should. Wendy would scold him; however he did work a lot at the lumberyard, the job not paying what it should for all the hard work he did, but she wished he would lay off the drinking.

She was grateful Shro accepted the responsibility of being a father to Eddie, her boy. She had made the mistake of sleeping with Vince thirteen years ago, back in high school. Good looks and a varsity jacket were all it took. Vince refused to wear a condom, using the "pull-out-before- you-ejaculate" method. Fail-safe, he would say. However, after he found out Wendy was pregnant, his thoughts changed. He even had the nerve to try and say, "Not my kid." When parents on both sides entered into the picture – and pressured Vince into a blood test to prove Eddie being Vince's child – poor Vince ended up working second shift down at Burgerville, a local fast food joint, to pay for the birth.

Instead of being a real father, acting as an adult and not a child, his days of employment and life ended when Vince decided to drink and drive his Camaro into the lake the very same night Wendy gave birth to Eddie. Supposedly Vince passed out before his car hit the water, drowning before emergency services showed up at the scene.

Wendy had barely placed the dishes down in front of two truckers, when the one with the bushy beard spoke up. "I ordered a baked potato instead of fries, ma'am."

"Sorry, sir. Let me get that fixed for you right quick." Wendy said, scooping up the plate and carrying it to the counter. She sat the plate down and flipped open her order pad. In her curly handwriting it clearly stated the trucker had indeed ordered a baked potato.

Gerald had probably done it on purpose, while flirting with her.

"Gerald!" she spat, walking up to the kitchen's window, making the two youngsters who were assisting Gerald in the kitchen wince and turn around. other cooks. "This order ain't right!"

"What are you talkin' about, sugar?"

Wendy hated when he called her that.

"This order ain't right. Fix it! See the ticket?" Wendy nearly shoved the ticket in Gerald's face.

Gerald popped a toothpick in his mouth, then looked at the ticket. "Let's see here. Oh. Okay. Well, hang on, hon." He took the plate, scraped the fries off onto the counter, and used tongs to pick up a potato wrapped in foil out of the oven and placed it on the plate. He handed the plate back to Wendy. "Oops."

"Gerald, that 'oops' could mean a poor tip."

"Hey, don't blame me if you can't be nice to people."

"I am nice."

"You're not bein' nice to me."

"You're the exception to the rule."

Gerald smiled. "I love it when you're angry."

Wendy glared at him, shook her head, walked off.

Her intentions of delivering the food and apologizing to the customer was short-lived when the lights went out.

Chapter 9

A chill ran down Rachael's spine as her mind tried to comprehend what she had witnessed. Nothing dead merely gets up and walks away — especially a human corpse. Sure, she'd seen horror flicks in her younger days, watching the dead rise from their graves and attack the living, stuff from movies, based on Stephen King novels.

Did she want to venture into the woods, maybe see if the boy had crawled in there? But how, if he was already dead?

She flipped open her phone. Dean's smiling face stared back at her through the "No Service" notice. Not a good sign. She decided to see if she had the flashlight in the back of the Honda. Hopefully Dean didn't take it out. Maybe she would venture in the dark, if she had light to see by.

She raised the hatch, fumbled around in the dark until she touched a screw driver, a tool box, jumper cables, and finally, the rubber surface of the flashlight. Using her thumb to switch it on, the beam sliced through the dark.

The flashlight's beam found a trail of blood leading away from the puddle, dropping off into a ditch, before the woods began.

"Oh, Geez..."

Rachael dry swallowed. She stepped toward the woods as her

foot slid down into the ditch. "Rach, whacha doin', girl? Lost your mind or something?" she asked aloud. She knew the right thing to do would be to get back into the Honda and go get help. But, as a nurse, was still obliged to see if she could help the kid.

Rachael trained the flashlight on the wet trees, passing them as she ventured further into the woods. Dead, wet leaves covered the ground, the cold air sending a shiver through her body. She wondered if the growing chill of fear brought her goose bumps as well. Trees held fresh blood seeping down the bark, leaving Rachael a path to follow. She glanced over her shoulder, and realized she had strayed fairly far from the road.

She heard a long moan. Hard to tell its direction.

"Is that you?" Rachael asked, moving the flashlight back and forth, its beam highlighting the trees and bushes and fallen leaves. "If it is, tell me where you are and I'll come to you. There's no need to be scared of me. I'm a nurse."

For a moment, silence. Then the drawn out moan returned to Rachael's ears. She thought it had come from another direction, away from the red path. She swung the flashlight.

Nothing.

The moan echoed through the trees, slowly melting into a laugh.

"Hello? Is somebody with you?"

A branch snapped. Rachael swung the flashlight.

Nothing.

"Where are you? Please, tell me, pl—whoa!" Something brush against her leg. "Hey!" Something else brushed against her hand holding the flashlight, and she almost dropped it.

She heard footsteps behind her.

The moan returned, included a giggle.

"Wh—what's going on?" Rachael frowned. Bit her bottom lip. Still, the flashlight's beam only shoved back the dark, revealed the woods.

Something brushed against her leg,

"Hey! Now, look!" Frustrated, she pushed away her fear: "Come out and show yourself! Shame on you for scaring someone! You hear me? Come out and show yourself!"

Laughter followed a louder moan. A strong wind blew, snapping away leaves, whipping through her hair, smacking her in the face.

Something knocked her face-first onto the cold ground. Her flashlight slipped out of her grip, rolling to a stop where the beam caught three pairs of child-sized tennis shoes.

She gazed up at three heads peering down at her. Her screams masked their giggling as knives cut into her.

Chapter 10

Dean hadn't heard from Rachael. Not good. He couldn't phone her and with the power out, he stumbled around the house, bumping into furniture. He located a flashlight, but the batteries were dead. So he lit a candle and sat it on the coffee table. The full moon added a little light to see by, its glow radiating through the front window.

He walked to the front window. Darkness lurked inside other houses on his street.

Dean opened the door, the cool air hit him in the face, and he stepped out onto the porch. Stepping closer to the street he noticed Shro's house, dark like his own, and the guy's truck parked out front. He wondered if he was home. Not exactly fond of the guy, he acknowledged him only when he had to with a wave.

Rather than leaving the house, venturing across the street, Dean slipped back inside. If the power didn't return soon he knew he might have to grab the kerosene heater out of the garage. However, since he didn't know if it still had fuel in it, venturing out to buy kerosene might be a bad idea. How much more of the town would be without power? Most of it? He probably wouldn't even be able to get any kerosene from any gas station close by.

Damned if driving thirty miles to find a gas station would be the only option.

So, Dean decided to get more food since his stomach started to growl. Perhaps the power would come back on soon. Ladling out his second spoonful of stew onto the plate, something moved in the backyard. Attempting to adjust his eyes to the darkness, he saw nothing. As close as the house was to the woods, he often spotted deer and other wildlife.

Yeah, that's all it could have been.

He walked back into the living room and sat down. He had only taken two bites when a shadow passed by the front window, startling him. Placing the plate on the coffee table, he rose, walked to the window and looked out.

Nothing.

He opened the front door again and stepped out onto the porch. He found nothing unusual. Drifting back into the house, he shook his head.

Only my imagination.

While he ate, he prayed Rachael was safe, never noticing the two eyes peeking through the kitchen window.

Chapter 11

Tall grass swayed back and forth in the vast field. The ground held the first body from the town of Hampshire, impaled, leaning to the side. The sacrifice twitched with what life still coursed through her blood, fighting a losing battle for the body to continue living.

They hadn't killed her in the woods.

And God she wished that they had.

When the knives slid into her cutting and ripping she screamed. She prayed someone would hear her. But she was all alone, feeling the knives do their work. Laughter and the giggling from children filled her ears. Voices she had once thought were pleasant to hear, something so fulfilling to an adult's heart, like watching a child's face light up on Christmas morning when the presents are ripped opened and the toys are found beneath the wrapping. In all of her life she never imagined a child could be so horrifying.

So cold.

Soon, she tasted the copper flavor of blood and her screaming gurgled. She prayed for death to come, for it to slip its cold hand into hers, and lead her into the afterlife. Though, it didn't arrive and the knives withdrew, leaving her with wounds leaking blood.

But she stayed alive.

Barely.

Rachael had been dragged over the woodland floor with gnarled roots scraping her back, until brought into a clearing. Her eyes watched the full moon look down at her, a peaceful silver orb in the sky.

She wanted to lay and gaze at the satellite and remember Dean's face before she died.

Pictures flipped through her mind. Memories of the first time the two had met, in a coffee shop listening to a jazz band. Three young musicians who could play Thelonious Monk, Charlie Parker, Toots Thielemans, Duke Ellington, and Benny Goodman had taken the stage. Almost as if the legends had risen from their graves, possessed the band members and performed in front of the crowd.

She had been a shy girl; Dean had been a shy boy. In a rather odd way, they had hit it off, even though they only had a few things in common.

Another few pictures flipped when Dean comforted her at the funeral home, after her parents were killed coming home from vacation. At the time, Rachael couldn't take off from college to go with them. She thought it would be nice if only the two of them went. Later, she wished she would have burned along with them as the car caught flame as it crashed head—on into the tractor trailer.

Before more pictures flashed, a terrible pain exploded through her lower back and ripped onward, to rest against the spine, then tear through the thin meat of her left shoulder. Near her left eye, a sharp tip of a wooden pole was wet with her blood. A plague of pain ravaged her nerves as it snaked through her body.

Rachael prayed for God to allow her the peace of death.

She felt herself rise up, her skin stretch and rip more, as the end of the pole was stuck into the soil. She was too numb to feel it when they eviscerated her and her intestines fell out, thumping the ground, steam rising from the pile.

The shadow, the evil entity, stood in her view, formed into a human-looking shape, black as night. It gazed at her. Five children, their eyes watching intently, their skin ash-gray, their lips pulled back in a toothy grin, all stood behind the entity.

The entity grinned.

The first sacrifice before the slaughter. The victim had to be impaled, disemboweled, the organs inside pulled free and dispersed on the ground in front in accordance with the sacred ritual.

Four hooded demons called The Reckoning implemented the rules, etching the words into stone. First blood is drawn upon each town or village before the slaughter. The world continued to shift toward the end. The entity's plans were moving forward, finishing the task.

Now, all they needed to complete the ritual: another sacrifice.

***

History Lesson

A drifter walked down the slope and entered Woodbin, a small village which would be renamed later as Woodbury. Villagers gave him a cautious eye. Others, who sold vegetables and fruit, did the same. Children ran and played, kicking a ball made out of rope. They, too, stopped and observed the stranger, then continued with their game.

A large sculpture of a bearded man stood in square, holding the Bible in the bend of his right arm, His left hand held a large sword, hung low. A stone crown sat atop his scalp and the long face gave a solemn look.

The drifter followed a path leading up to a castle. Two guards armed with swords halted him.

"What do you want, drifter?" one asked.

"I am here to see the king," the drifter replied. "I have urgent business with him."

"What kind of business?"

"Please, it is very important. I must speak with the king at once. There is terror coming from the hills. Your village will soon be under attack."

The guard turned to the other, frowned, and then returned to Kabul. "What terror do you speak of? If it is an army, we are a solid force. We will not be beaten."

"Please, I beg of you; allow me to speak with your king. I will not deny your army is great, but this is a different matter. Something will take this village by storm."

The guard scratched his stubbly chin.

"Please I beg of you, in the name of God, our Father."

"All right," he huffed after a few more minutes. "Come this way."

Only one guard guided the drifter through a large wooden door and into a massive hallway made of stone. Then he was escorted through a wooden door and down a hallway with columns running along each side. Between them, an open view on one side overlooked the village. The scene on the other side displayed snow-covered mountains, far away.

When they arrived at the next door the guard opened it, letting it swing wide. Torches were lit which ran around the diameter of the walls. A large painting of angels fighting winged demons sat right above where the king sat on his throne.

The guard fell to one knee, bowing before his king, raised his head. "I have a visitor here to see you, M'Lord."

The statue in the village had portrayed this king well, though he had grown much older and much fatter since it had been sculpted. The ruler of Woodbin reached over to grab a bottle of wine and the gold rings on his fingers tapped against the glass.

"What business do you have with me, drifter?" A hoarse, though firm voice of a leader.

"M'Lord, I am Kabul. Regretfully, I bring you bad news from

the west. It is terror."

"Terror, you say? What kind of terror?" He cleared his throat, reached over, and plucked four grapes out of a bowl.

Kabul swallowed. "Rats, sir. They have taken over small villages, eaten their fruits and vegetables, lapped up their wine, ran amuck, terrorizing women and children"

"Rats? Ha! Why would they be so bad? That is not terror. We can manage those little creatures ourselves."

"M'Lord, we are talking tens of thousands of them. Not a few."

The king chuckled. "How can there be tens of thousands?"

"What I say is true, M'Lord. I beg of you. Please believe me."

"If it is a pest problem, you say, we will take care of this."

"M'Lord, I am trying to save you the anguish of this terror."

The king sighed deeply. "If this is your bad news, we will control it. If it was an army of men, we would fight to the death. We would crush them!" He made a fist.

"This, M'Lord, will be the same thing."

"Ahh!" The king turned his head, waved away this nonsense using his hand. "This is not bad news! Guards! Take this drifter out of my sight!"

"B-but, M'Lord," Kabul begged as guards dragged him away. Before they opened the door to enter into the hall, he added, "You will be sorry you did not listen, M'Lord!"

Escorted outside and told to leave the village and to never return, Kabul watched at a safe distance from Woodbin, waiting for the horror to arrive.

Two days passed before a black mass full of venom swarmed out of the hills and entered the streets of the village, spreading disease. Kabul could hear the screams of the villagers, young and old, fearing for their lives. Guards from the castle killed some of the beasts, stabbing them with their swords and knives, but had a very hard time controlling their fury of clawing and biting.

Kabul let this go on a full day before he walked back to the village, watching rats scurry everywhere, burrowing in fruits and vegetables. Women screamed at the sight of the rodents and children were chased by the small beasts.

Kabul withdrew a musical pipe from a pouch at his side, walked to the center of the village by the statue of the king, lifted the instrument to his lips, and began to play a tune. Soon, it reached the ears of the villagers, reached the small ears of the rats, making them stop in their tracks. The rats sniffed the air, their little ears perked up.

Kabul left the village with a stream of rats following in his wake, leading them into the hills, as if it swallowed him and the rats.

No one knew where he led the creatures but when Kabul stepped a foot back into Woodbin the next day villagers young and old all ran up to him, proclaiming him a savior of their village. A true hero.

Even though Kabul had saved Woodbin, the king was not pleased. He did not want another savior nor some drifter who was a hero of the village. The king had earned his honor a very long time ago as warrior and commander, leading wars against men for this land. He made Woodbin his own, creating a safe environment. Let not some nasty drifter from the hills come and be a savior in a single day's time! He did not want any of his people to give glory to anyone but himself, their king.

Two guards were ordered by the king to collect Kabul. They pushed through the crowd of villagers who praised him and told Kabul the king called for him. Gladly, he accompanied them. He could now prove the king wrong, not taking heed to the warning.

However, when he arrived inside the castle the doors slammed shut and he was forced into the dungeon.

"Drifter, did I not tell you to not return?" the king said.

"M'Lord, I came and helped your village. I saved your people from despair of the rats. Why are you doing this to me?"

The king admired as the drifter lay helpless, tied down on a torturing rack. "Because there can only be one savior in Woodbin. One hero who fought for this land long ago, and made this village what it is. Call me selfish if you will, but I cannot allow another drifters to stroll into my village, saving it, thinking he or she wished a reward."

"A reward?" Kabul asked, taken aback. "I do not wish anything for my services, M'Lord. I do not need gold or material to make me happy. I wish to help people."

The king frowned, scratched his chin. "You mean to tell me you have no use for gold, then? Or even treasures from faraway lands?"

"No, M'Lord. I do not."

The king had acquired so much gold and treasure over the years it filled the other half of the huge dungeon. Not even the villagers knew of its existence.

"Well. I guess I was wrong about you. I would have thought you would have accepted gifts."

"I do, at times. I accept food if I am hungry or a place to rest if I am weary."

"Mmmph." The king dug a large red apple out of his pocket, gazed at it, and took a bite. "Shocking. I have never met someone like you. We've had strangers come into Woodbin, begging for food and shelter. Of course, they were turned away. We are a quiet village and do not like outsiders. They bother me."

"M'Lord, your people seem to have no problem with me. Can you not see I saved you and your people from the invasion of the rats?"

The king took another bite, chewed, but didn't swallow as he nonchalantly said, "No. Maybe someone like yourself who can lead the rats away, brought them. A lone drifter like you is capable of, say, playing notes on that musical pipe of yours to lure those rats into villages. I think the word I am looking for is...treachery! Manipulating innocent people!"

"M'Lord! I would never do such a thing! I beg of you! Pleas

belie—"

"As I said, it is because there must never be another hero and warrior of Woodbin. There's really no room for such stupidity. Guard!" His eyes found the one who held his hand on the wheel to make the torture rack commence. "Proceed with the execution while I enjoy watching his flesh being stretched and ripped from his bones."

It is said Kabul's guttural screams could be heard for miles. Villagers winced at his horror, holding their children tight, covering their ears from the sounds.

Kabul dead, they pulled what was left of him off the rack and wiped up the spilled blood and discarded the corpse into a nearby lake.

Upon his death Kabul's soul lifted up into a bright white light delivering him inside a long stone passageway bathed in a light yellow glow. However, things became oddly dark with shadows dancing on both sides of him. Kabul figured he was on the way to the afterlife, and hoped to see his beloved and the children. And he was right, to an extent. His soul did not quite stay on course to the Pearly Gates, but was diverted to Purgatory before he could arrive in Heaven.

Kabul knew of Purgatory, a place where one undergoes purification to achieve the holiness necessary to enter the joy of Heaven. Brought to a wooden door where it swung open by itself, unveiling a long hallway full of closed doors, two hands grabbed hold, preventing him to move forward.

A voice, gravelly and old, spoke to him out of the dark. It asked if he felt that vengeance was needed for what Woodbin had done to him.

Kabul, with fire even in the heart of his soul, did not speak of it at first.

Asked again, the voice explained it knew he wanted to take revenge. It knew of Kabul's anger, his hate for the selfish king. How can a weak, insecure mortal do this to him? How can a mortal take pleasure killing another over such prejudice and jealousy? It added Kabul died for nothing. His time on Earth had come abrupt. It was not his time to die yet.

Kabul stated wished he could take revenge on the king as well as the people of the village. They stood by and allowed Kabul to die. They were as responsible as the king.

The voice acknowledged Kabul to be patient. At least for now. He would be returned to Earth yet, able to seek revenge. The voice assured Kabul, upon the death of the king, the ruler would be dealt with by a quartet of demons called The Reckoning.

Then the voice asked how Kabul knew of the rats invading the land.

Kabul stood there and did not speak for a very long while. When he did, he suddenly had no idea how he knew of the rats. He also had no recollection of when the thought arrived in his head. His brain could not produce it. He asked the voice if it could have possibly been black magic that informed him.

The voice said no, and did not further investigate why Kabul knew of the rat problem. It knew the answer, but did not say, holding back the truth: The warning of the invading pests had been injected into his dreams one night by the Devil himself to stir up trouble, in which the Dark One succeeded in doing so. It was almost like a variation of what the Devil told Adam and Eve while they were in the Garden of Eden, tricking her into eating an apple.

Horror washed across his vision as his previous duties as Good switched to a forthcoming Evil during his long wait in the depths of Hell. Demons molded him into what he has become today, an evil entity. A shadow carrying the cold blood of death and revenge.

Now, in the deep darkness of the night, The Reckoning watches.

Chapter 12

The television shut off in the middle of one of Barry's favorite episodes of the *Twilight Zone*, "Night Call", leaving him with only the glow of the fireplace throwing shadows on the white walls, illuminating the pictures of his mother.

Barry had managed to pull himself off the kitchen floor, stumble back into the living room, land in his recliner and throw the footrest up. The handle on the side lay defunct. Barry made a point to not fix it, being far easier to sit down and have the footrest act on its own accord.

Barry watched in his drunken haze as the flames crackled and licked the sides of the brick walls leading up through the chimney. The only heat in the house, since the furnace broke years ago, he made it the only room where he ate and slept; unless he had to "go potty".

He sighed, took a deep breath, reached down, and grabbed the bottle of whiskey. He let the burn coat his throat again, and instead of sitting the bottle down, let it dangle, holding onto the tip between two knuckles.

Power had gone out from time to time around Hampshire, normally he sat and waited for it to return. During the wait, the unpleasant memory slowly surfaced of his mother telling him in her drug-induced voice whenever the lights do go out, God is letting us know it is mother and son time.

Barry's eyes drifted over to the picture of his mother above the fireplace, watching as the glow of the fire accented his mother's pale face. Her blue eyes peered out of the picture at Barry, finding her son. Her mouth, only a slit, stretched into half a smile.

A door creaked open in Barry's mind, and the ghostly voice of his mother – the lullaby she always sung to him in her sweet voice – leaked out, long before the addiction to the drugs:

Hush little baby don't say a word,
Momma's gonna buy you a mockingbird.
And if that mockingbird don't sing,
Momma's gonna buy him a diamond ring.

A tear slipped from Barry's eye. He missed his mother dearly. He wished he could have turned back time

He stood, stumbled, but regained his balance and stared at his mother's picture. Her eyes, thoughts of her presence still in the house or her smell sunk into the furniture, saturated in the air, returned the nightmares of his youth.

What he wanted—needed—was another release of built up pressure; a stress reliever. Something tearing his mind away from thinking of his mother. Thoughts of under the sheets with her.

He craned his neck toward the backyard, in the darkness of the woods, focusing in the direction where the graves were. He missed having play time with those children. How he eluded the Law, he would never know. Maybe luck. Maybe because he picked the kids up in the big city up north when their parents weren't looking and brought them back here to have play time.

He fell down on his knees and sat the bottle down. How long had it been?

Months?

Days?

When was the last time when he took a playmate?

He hung his head, started to drift off.

And his demons arrived.

A courtroom. The jury sat to the left, all gathered together to unite and make a decision on Barry's future. The judge, a haggard old man with deep set hazel eyes and leathery skin, sat behind the bench with his eyes crawling over a lonely Barry who sat behind a wooden table. The plaintiff, a tall woman, the lawyer, all business in her expression, sat behind her own table.

"Mrs. Walsh, please proceed," the judge said to the lady in a deep tone echoing off the walls.

"The court calls Sammy to the witness stand," Ms. Walsh said.

Two doors swung open in back and for the first time, as Barry looked over his shoulder, he noticed a large crowd who consisted of all women, young and old. Every one of their faces glared at the defendant.

A small boy entered the courtroom, carrying a teddy bear almost as tall as he, trailing pieces of dried up mud all the way to the witness stand. There, he placed his grimy palm on a thick Bible in front of him.

The judge's eyebrows lifted and he said with a smile, "Do you swear to tell the truth, the whole truth, so help you God?"

"Yes, your honor. And hope to die."

Low laughter spread through the crowd, and the judge told Ms. Walsh to proceed.

She walked up and asked, "Sammy, do you remember what happened on July 6, 2002?"

The boy's small face, filthy with dirt, also missed one eye. "Yes, ma'am."

"Could you tell the court what happened on the playground the day of July 6?"

"A big man came up to me while I played on the slide wearing that clown costume." He pointed to a costume spread out, sitting on a table. A red wig sat beside it.

"Let the records show Exhibit A."

The clerk typed it into her laptop.

"So, what did the man tell you?"

"He said my momma was hurt."

"How did this make you feel, Sammy?"

"Scared." His little hands squeezed his teddy bear.

"Did the man want you to follow him?"

"Yes."

"Can you point him out to me?"

The boy clutched the teddy bear.

"Sammy, please point to the man who did this to you. Remember, he can't hurt you anymore."

Sammy lowered the teddy bear. "There! He pointed at Barry, "That man right there!"

Walsh turned, gave Barry a mean look, and the judge said, "Let the records show the court recognizes Barry Freckles."

The court clerk typed it into her laptop.

"Now, Sammy," Walsh continued, "where did you go with Barry?"

"Uncle Barry took me to his car and told me he was going to drive me to the hospital to see my momma."

"Uncle Barry?"

"That's what he told me to call him."

"Oh. I see." Walsh glared at the pedophile, then, to Sammy: She asked: "But he did not drive you to the hospital, right?"

"No, ma'am."

"Please tell the court where Mr. Freckles — Uncle Barry — took you."

Sammy paused, squeezing the life out of the teddy bear, gazing at Barry.

Barry looked at him in horror. Not only one eye missing, but the other had vanished.

"H—He drove me to his house and said he had a room full of toys I could play with. He said little kids can't go upstairs to the intensof, intensuv, inensif—"

"Intensive care unit?"

"Yeah, that's it."

Low laughter rang through the crowd behind Barry.

"Uncle Barry said he would go check on my mom himself."

"He took you to his house, told you he had a room full of toys, and then said he would leave and go check on your mom?"

"Yes, ma'am."

The clerk's fingers typed quickly.

"Sammy, did Uncle Barry leave?"

"Only for a few minutes or so, while Barry took me to the room with a lot of toys. There were a lot of girl-toys. Not anything a boy would want to play with."

"Such as?"

"Dolls of all shapes and sizes."

"Really?"

"Yep."

"So, when Uncle Barry returned, what happened?"

"Well, he sat down beside me and rubbed my leg. I told him not to, but he kept doing it."

Barry caught the sight of Sammy's face peeling back, flaking onto the floor, exposing a crimson shade changing to an ash-gray color. Barry swallowed. *Were others in the courtroom seeing this?*

"So, you told him to refrain from touching your leg, and he didn't stop?" Walsh's foot stepped on a piece of discarded skin.

"Yeah."

"What else happened?"

Sammy sighed deeply. "He led me outside into the woods. He told me he wanted to show me something."

"Did he?"

"Yep." Sammy chuckled. "He showed me the hole where he was going to bury me."

A gasp rang through the crowd.

"Really? He told you that?"

"Yup." Sammy's mouth started bleeding, dripping off his chin.

"If we were to take a trip to Uncle Barry's house could you show me, and the court, where he buried you?"

"Sure."

The judge slammed down his gavel, startling Barry, and said, "A half hour recess and we meet behind Mr. Freckles' house." He looked at Sammy and smiled. "You may step down, young man."

"Okay." Sammy slid off the chair gripping his teddy bear and left another trail of dirt mixed with droplets of blood and flesh on the floor when he walked over to Barry. "You're gonna be sorry, mister! You are gonna *be sorry!*" His voice rose and echoed in the courtroom.

Barry swallowed hard. He sighed, stood up, turned and saw the many different faces staring at him, already judging him: a pedophile, a murderer. A boy who had sexual relations with his own mother. Barry knew their thoughts shouted for him to die. Not a quick death, a lethal injection or frying in the electric chair – No, too easy. They would rather watch a death with the noose tight against your throat, your body dangling from a thick tree limb as they witnessed you take your last breath.

Barry saw their faces. He knew it's what they wanted.

He blinked and found himself in the woods behind his house. Six empty graves, – opened wounds in the earth, – lay in front of him. Trees had been cleared and the entire courtroom sat there. The judge sat behind the bench, the jury to the side, and the clerk on a stool with her computer in her lap. Walsh suddenly appeared out of thin air, from Barry's left.

"Now, Sammy, where is the exact place where you were buried?"

Walsh asked.

Sammy entered into the right side of Barry's vision, turned his black-haired head to look at him with his missing eyes, grinning a sharp-toothed grin, and pointed to a spot directly at his feet.

"Right there?" Walsh asked.

"Yes, ma'am," Sammy replied.

"Let the record show where the grave had been dug," the judge said. "And, where Sammy has been buried."

Through all of this, Barry had no recollection of this child. He remembered other children, but not Sammy. Had he killed so many he hadn't kept track?

"Mr. Freckles," the judge said.

He turned, faced the judge. "Yes, Your Honor." Walsh had disappeared. Sammy stood by the judge.

"Your actions of murder in the first degree give me no choice. I sentence you to death for murdering and burying Sammy."

"But, judge, I didn't do it! I— I don't remember this child!" Barry pleaded. Behind him, he heard a familiar voice.

"Barry! My dear, dear, little Barry!"

He turned and saw his mother dressed in the same flowered dress she had been buried in. Her arms were open, offering him an embrace.

"No! Get away from me!" Barry spat, his eyes wide with fear.

Shoved from behind, he stumbled and fell into the same hole where Sammy had rested. Before he rose his mother ripped away her dress and jumped down and pushed him back and straddled him. Her arms split into tentacles, the tips poking, touching her son's face and body. "There, there, my little Barry," she whispered, "Love your momma, Barry, love her so special!"

Dirt began to fall from above and cascade off his face. He saw Walsh holding the shovel. "Nighty-night, Mr. Freckles. Sleep tight. Don't let the maggots and worms bite."

She held her head back and cackled and continued to throw

down more dirt. Sammy stood on the edge, grinning with a bleeding surface of a face. Barry's mother who had once had soft skin and a beautiful face with blue eyes and long dark hair had turned into a monstrosity: Flailing tentacles to molest his body; black flesh stretched over her body, riddled with maggots; and an acrid stench of decay as her lips closed over his, her forked tongue probing, pushing entry for a loving, open-mouthed kiss ...

Something pulled Barry from his nightmare, shuffling in the darkness of the kitchen.

And giggled.

Chapter 13

"Eddie?" Dean asked, caught off guard as he observed the silhouette standing in the kitchen. "Is that you? Is everything okay at your house?" Dean saw the white Punisher emblem on the child's shirt and recognized Shro's stepson.

Had he not locked the backdoor? No big thing. They never had any trouble with thieves in Woodbury, anyway. Over the years he had heard stories on the news the crime rate skyrocketing in the larger cities. You did not worry with it here. Out here was country. People could breathe clean air, sit on their front porch and watch the stars at night. The only sounds you heard were the sounds of the night. The sounds of roaring of buses, busy streets, crowds of people talking and walking to and fro, or police sirens wailing did not intrude on the peace here.

"That you, Eddie?" Dean repeated.

The white skull emblem faded into the dark as the figure took a step back.

"Yeah. Can you come over to my house?" His voice was low. "Something happened."

"What happened? Shro okay? Your mom okay?"

Eddie asked, "Can you come over? Please? Something bad has

happened."

"Yeah. Sure thing. Hang on, kiddo. I'll get my coat." Dean pulled out a thick coat from the living room closet. Starting toward the backdoor, it hung open, and cool air caressed his face.

"Eddie! Wait up, champ!"

Dean picked up the pace. The wind whipped through his hair. He didn't think it had been as cold earlier when he had stepped out on the porch.

Rounding the corner, Dean saw the boy scurrying away, running in his white Sketcher tennis shoes toward the front door of his house, slipping inside. The wind caught the screen door, preventing it to close.

A horrible feeling curled inside Dean's gut. He hoped Eddie's parents were okay. He wondered if Shro's wife, Wendy, worked tonight at the truck stop. He found this out when he stopped in there one day to buy a Coke. The very thought of the place gave him a sour stomach. Not the finest diner in the area. The clientele and food went together what flowed through sewer pipes.

Shro's old truck sat there in front of the house, an eyesore of Hampshire with the paint peeling and a huge dent in the tailgate. Whenever Shro started it up, smoke would billow out of the exhaust.

Dean didn't notice Shro in the passenger seat, passed out in his drunken stupor.

When he entered the house, he noticed the broken lamp on the floor in the living room. "Eddie?" he asked. "Where you at?"

No response, only the yawning darkness of the house smelling of leftover dinner.

Dean stepped around the broken lamp. He barely made out the shapes of the couch, the chair and another lamp, unbroken, on an end table. The curtains in the front window were pulled back.

A loud thump from upstairs.

"Eddie? What the hell is going on?" Dean shouted. "Are you up there? Are you hurt?"

A moan, from the kitchen.

Turning a corner Dean saw a flicker of light dance on the kitchen's wall. He walked through the house, cursing, when his knee hit something. Stepping inside the kitchen his fingers touched a wet wall. Quickly he drew them away, looked, stopping in mid-step.

He gasped.

Blood.

His eyes followed the lonely candle on the counter, illuminating the sitter, Carolyn, who sprawled out on the floor face down, moaning with a halo of blood.

"Oh my God! Carolyn?" He knelt down, turned her over. Her young face and hair were crimson.

"Jesus!" he whispered.

Carolyn gasped, blood oozed out of the slice in her throat, bubbling. Her lips moved, trying to pronounce a word through wet blood. She held out one arm to Dean and began to say "H—help m—" before her eyes rolled to the left and the last of what life she held inside of her young body disappeared.

Dean stood there, shaken. *The hell happened here? Where was Eddie?* "Eddie? Eddie! Tell me where you are!"

His voice rang through the house.

Upstairs, the loud lump repeated.

Dean, now frantic and worried for Eddie — poor Eddie who came by sometimes while Dean worked outside on the lawn and chatted of Marvel superheroes of the past. Shro never took interest in comics, only in his hunk of junk in the garage.

Picking up the candle he made a dash from the kitchen, bumped into the wall, found the stairs, took them in threes and stopped on the landing. There were three bedrooms.

A low voice reached his ears.

"Eddie?"

The voice grew louder, bleeding into a cry, emanating from one bedroom.

Dean sprinted over to the door and kicked it open.

Eddie stood inside the room. The curtains over his window were open, the moon bathing the walls silver. His head tipped forward. His eyes glared at his bed. Shapes of superheroes fought the forces of evil on the bedspread and posters of horror flicks and sci-fi movies filled the walls. Some of the posters had been torn in half, littered the floor, while others had strips curled down, not yet free of their attachment on the wall.

"Eddie?" Dean whispered.

Eddie's head swiveled in the direction of Dean's words, his left eye peered at the man, and tears streamed down both cheeks. "No one wants to play with me anymore, Mr. Clemins."

Dean swallowed. "Wh—what's going on here?"

A grin stretched under Eddie's nose. "No one wants to play with me anymore Mr. Clemins."

"Eddie, what happened to Carolyn?"

The boy did not respond.

Dean took a step forward, his foot slipping in something wet. Eddie's door swung behind Dean holding a corpse on the coat hooks.

"Good God! Dean shouted, turning around to face the corpse. "Sc—Scooter?"

Scooter's mouth ajar, showed missing teeth. His eyes were no better, dug out by small hands. The inside of his gut exposed, his entrails, bloody worms, trailed out from his abdomen, reaching for the floor.

Dean's vision focused on Scooter. He wanted to tear it away, but could not, shocked at the revelation. As he drew in another breath Eddie slammed into him, knocking it out of his chest.

"Play with me, Mr. Clemins! Play with me!" Eddie's laughter shrilled through the house and the butcher knife he held glimmered in the moonlight.

Chapter 14

Eddie's shrill laugh leaked outside and woke Shro up. Shro really had no idea what he had been dreaming, but he thought it had been a good one. And his bladder ached.

The world had stopped spinning for Shro, replaced with a hammer pounding the top of his head. He sighed, wiped his face, and, after a few moments, opened the truck door.

And fell out onto the grass.

"Dammit!" he spat. He rolled over on his knees, stood up, and the hammer returned for another hit.

He cursed.

The front screen door banged against the frame with the wind.

The hell is Scooter? He was supposed to come back and get him after he checked out the place. Maybe the man was flirtin' with Carolyn. No. Shouldn't think that way. He shook his head. *Kinda disgustin there, Shro.*

Carolyn's car sat in the driveway. Shro could see his garage door open. Had he shut it before he left this morning before going to work? *Eddie better not have left it open, showing everyone on the block his diamond in the rud. Rut? Or was it rough? Hell, he couldn't remember.* He didn't want anyone nosing around the 'Cuda until he fixed it up and drove it out of the garage, his hand on the wheel, showing off his prize possession to everyone in Hampshire.

Shro stumbled to his house. Before stepping inside he stopped, unzipped, and pissed on the lawn. Once he set a foot in, he damn near slipped on the broken lamp.

The laughter returned, a reminder to Shro what had woke him up, as well as a loud thump right above his head.

Eddie's room.

What the devil is the child up to now? One day he had heard a commotion and ran upstairs to find Eddie jumping and doing rolls on the floor, fighting imaginary enemies. He scolded him, telling him to stop it or he wouldn't sit down for a week. Eddie obeyed. Shro even offered for the boy to accompany him into the garage to work on the 'Cuda, which the boy gladly declined.

Did Eddie already forget what I told him not to do?

He stumbled through the house, flicking light switches bringing no light. He went into the kitchen, slid on something, caught himself by grabbing the counter, cursed, and then found the drawer he needed. He opened it and reached inside for a flashlight. When he hit the button, the light instantly found Carolyn.

"Holy shit!" Shro spat and backed up. He kept the light on the young lady, saw all of the blood and the trail of red footprints.

He swung the light back to the bloody scene.

Was the girl dead? She couldn't be…right?

Carolyn's blue eyes had rolled to the side. Her mouth gaped open. Dried blood caked her lips. Shro's brain took a Kodak picture and tucked it away in one of the slots in his mind. In his younger days as a kid spotted a dead dog in the woods. Though comparison between human and animal is not actually the same, it reminded Shro of death.

And, he had never seen a human corpse before.

Following a trail of footsteps using the flashlight's beam, he climbed the stairs.

Another loud thump from Eddie's room.

"Eddie? Wha—what are you doin' in there, boy?" he stammered.

Shro's stepson did not respond.

"Eddie? You're not Superman, so quit jumping off the bed."

The door to Eddie's room flew open. Dean stumbled out, ran into Shro and they both tumbled down the stairs. The flashlight left Shro's grip and bounced down with the two men.

Eddie stood on the landing above, holding the butcher knife in his hand, peering down at the two adults who were trying to regain their composure.

"More playmates!" Eddie cried.

Chapter 15

The power out, Wendy wormed her way back to the front counter, bumping into a pair of customers who were trying to leave. Turned to apologize, and spun back around, face first into Gerald. Or at least that's who it smelled like – grease and sweat.

"Dammit!" she spat.

"Sorry, Wendy, thought I'd come out from the kitchen to see what's up."

"We're all in the dark, that's what's up! We have no power. Is there by chance a back-up generator in this place?"

Gerald moved a toothpick from one corner of his mouth to the other. "Can't recall. Jerry never mentioned it."

"You're the boss on staff and you don't have a clue if we have a generator?"

"Nope."

"What the hell good are ya?" She did not want to be in the dark without power; especially around Gerald or any of the truckers who wanted to cop a feel. The other waitress, Laura, enjoyed flirting with the customers and didn't mind getting goosed in the behind. She always said it encouraged tips.

Gerald did not reply back,

Headlights turned on, the flick of a switch, out by the pumps, cutting through the dark and through the front window. Three different vehicles took off. Someone ran out, shouting after them. Wendy noticed it being the clerk who worked the register over on the other side, in the convenient store.

"Come back and pay your bills!" the woman shouted.

"Whoa! Julie over there's pissed!" Gerald said.

"No doubt," Wendy added. "Stupid. Leaving without paying."

Gerald agreed.

"So," Wendy returned to the conversation at hand, "No back-up generator?"

"Don't know," Gerald replied.

"Well, can you call our fearless leader and ask him?"

Gerald paused, replied, "Fearless leader?"

"Jerry?"

"Oh, sure, hang on a sec." He walked over to the phone on the wall and found it dead when he placed it to his ear. "Huh. No dial tone."

"Got a cell phone handy?"

"Nope. Don't carry one."

"Great. Mine was disconnected last month." Wendy ran a hand through her hair.

"Oh."

"What about Robert and Gary? They have one?"

"Hey boys, either of you got a cell we can use?" Gerald shouted through the dark.

"What?" Robert's voice came from behind Wendy, startling her. She twisted around to face him. He held a lit cigarette lighter. "What do you want?" he asked.

Gary walked up, joining the group.

"Oh," Gerald said, "thought you two were back there."

"Hell no! We aren't stayin' back there in the dark! Ever seen those roaches we have? They're huge!"

"We don't have any roaches, Roberr!"

"Sure we do. Gary's seen them, too. Right, man?"

"Yep!" Gary agreed.

"Hey! Don't say that too loud!" Gerald snapped under his breath. "Don't want any of these customers hearin' it!"

"What's it matter, man? It's not the place is elegant and pricy and luxurious and fancy and—"

"I get the point, Robert," Gerald said as he shook his head. "Look, do either of you have a cell phone?"

Robert chuckled. So did Gary.

"What? What's so damn funny?"

"Man, Gerald," Robert replied, "It's like askin' us if we're wearin' our underwear. We never leave home without it, dude."

"Yeah." Gary added.

"Okay," Wendy said, "then, can we borrow one to call Jerry?"

"Geez, don't have to be so rude, Wendy." Gary informed her.

"I'm not!"

"Yes you are." He shook his head.

"Look." She sighed. "I'm sorry but it seems you two think this is all fun and games."

"No, we really don't," Robert told her.

"Sorry, Wendy." Gary reached into his pocket. "Here, I have a cellphone."

"That's fine, Gary," Wendy replied. "Thank you."

Gary handed his phone to Gerald who began tapping in numbers.

"What the hell happened, Wendy?" Gary said. "What's up with the power goin' out?"

"Damned if I know," she told him.

"Hey... hey, Jerry?" Gerald said, turning his huge body around, facing away from the other three. "Do you know if you have a gener...Jerry? Still there? Jerry?" He pulled the phone away from his ear, switched back around, and screwed his face up in confusion. "It says no service."

"What?" Gary said. "My parents paid my bill. What the hell's up with that?"

"Hard telling," Wendy said. "Could have forgotten to send it, Robert," she said as she thought, *must be nice to have your own phone bill paid every month.*

"Ain't no way. They always pay for it."

"Bet they do, in more ways than one."

"What?"

"Nothing. Yours have service, Robert?"

Robert hadn't flipped his phone open yet, when he did, he frowned at the screen. "Damn! No service. Something wrong with the towers not picking up the signal?"

"I don't know. Do we have a flashlight in this place?"

"Think so. But they're, er, back in the kitchen."

"Would you go and check?"

Robert swallowed. "I, I guess so."

"Thanks, Robert," Wendy said.

"Watch the roaches, dude." Gary said after him.

Gerald gave him a dirty look.

"What the shit's goin' on here, honey?"

Wendy turned to face an older man holding a lit cigarette lighter, outfitted in blue jeans and a jacket to match. His hat said Oldman's Trucking Company. "I don't know, sir. We're trying to find out if this place has a back-up generator."

"Where's the boss?"

"Right here," Wendy pointed to Gerald, "but he doesn't know much and we're having trouble callin' the manager."

"How come?"

"There's no service on the cell phones we're trying to use."

The old guy reached inside of his coat, took out his cell and flipped it open. "Well, frog shit." he said after a second or two. "Ain't got no service neither."

"I was afraid you'd say that," Wendy's said.

"Look, me and a few of the other guys could pull our rigs around and flash our headlights through the front window. Give us better light to see by. At least 'til the power gets back on."

Wendy let the words sink in. "Good idea, sir."

"I'll git right on it, honey."

"At least *someone* has a good idea." Wendy sighed, shooting Gerald a sideways glance. "Yeah," Gerald agreed.

A voice came across the diner. "Hey, is our food free tonight since we can't see to eat this slop?"

"No. It's not," Gerald said.

"Aw, give a guy a break!" Someone else chimed in. "Would it be too much to ask?"

"Times are tight, and I ain't the owner."

"He'll never know."

"Sure he will. We have to count the money at the end of the shift to see if we're short or not. The big boss'll know if there's money missin'."

"So. Doesn't apply to me. I'm only a customer."

"Yes it does. Don't try leavin' without payin'!"

"You gonna stop me?"

Gerald didn't reply back. If Jerry wanted him to be a thug, he needed to pay him more on the hour. Piss on trying to fight someone.

"Thought so," the voice said as the sound of a chair slid across the floor, footsteps, then the front door opening, and Gerald watched the guy leave.

Wendy had been prepared for the whole place to get up and follow the guy's lead. But nothing happened. As soon as someone else started to speak, his words were drowned out by the noise of a tractor and trailer pulling around from the back lot, fifteen feet from the front window, shining its beams through the glass. Another followed close behind.

Heads and shoulders of the customers were caught in the

illumination.

"Nice of the old guy to this," Wendy said.

"Yeah," Robert said. A beam projected from the flashlight he held.

"Good! You found one. Guess you can shut it off. We need to conserve the batteries."

"Oh, okay." Robert shut off the flashlight and reached in his pocket, pulled out his smokes, knocked one free, and lit up.

"Hey, you know you can't smoke in here," Wendy said.

"Desperate times calls for desperate measures, Wendy. I need to feed my nicotine crave."

"Put it out, Robert," Gerald told him.

"C'mon, dude. I need a fix!"

"Put it out. Now."

Robert took a long drag and dropped the butt into a glass of water.

"Thank you," Gerald said. He glanced at Wendy, eyeing her body.

Wendy turned, noticed him staring.

"Lookin' mighty fine in the headlights, Wendy."

"You mean like a deer or something? Callin' me some wild animal living in the woods?"

"You're a wild one, aren't ya?"

"Shut up, Gerald. Get your mind back to what's happening here."

Gerald's smile never left his face. He opened his mouth to add another flirtatious remark when the old guy wearing the Oldman's Trucking Company cap said something, turning everyone's attention outside.

Small figures stepped in front of the headlights, throwing long shadows.

"Who the hell are they?"

"Damned if I know. A group of kids, I suppose."

Chapter 16

While the evil began to prosper in Hampshire, Martha slept. She had gone to bed only a few hours ago, right after reading a passage out of the book of Revelations from the Bible. She never, ever, went to bed without reading from the Good Book. She always said her prayers at night, praying to God to take good care of her Frank in Heaven. She would even mention to God to please not allow any other beautiful women who were in Heaven to flirt with her handsome Frank. It would give her a chuckle, too.

After reading from Revelations, the thoughts of the end of world scared her. She could not imagine all of God's creation obliterated from the face of the Earth. The very thought of Satan himself rising from the sea with ten heads and seven horns was ghastly and frightening. But she felt if it did happen, her soul belonged to the Almighty Father's.

Her destination: the Pearly White Gates.

Martha was pulled out of a pleasant dream by a sound downstairs. Her eyes flipped open. She lay there a minute. The sound came again. Something fell, sounding like glass shattering.

She hoped that she was still dreaming. She feared that of all things there could actually be a burglar in house.

But after she heard voices, fear oozed into her pores.

Her first thought: call the police. She reached for the phone, placed it to her ear, but found it dead. With her finger she pushed 911, hoping to hear a dial tone, which did not come.

Grabbing the end table for leverage for her petite frame, she swung her legs around, feet dangling well above the carpet. She tried to turn on a lamp only to find it not working.

She allowed her legs to drop down. She picked up her small frames and placed them on her nose. Her back spoke to her, letting her know it stiff as a board. Good old Arthur, short for arthritis, let her know he still lived in her joints.

A shuffling sound came from downstairs, sending a chill across the back of her neck.

Frank had bought a shotgun and a rifle almost ten years before he died: the Browning Auto-5 and the Winchester Model 70 Super Shadow. He used to shoot targets and even hunted, preferring the Winchester. They were both locked up in the gun cabinet in the hallway.

Martha had promised both guns to a young man who went to her church. She always seemed to forget to take them. Hopefully, the early stages of Alzheimer weren't setting in.

Martha did not enjoy the thought of a gun being present in her house. She sure didn't approve of it when Frank came home holding the shotgun, showing it off to her and their neighbor next door, and an avid hunter. But, being a good wife, she didn't spoil Frank's fun. He had never told her she could not take a trip out of town with the ladies from church when she wanted to. And never told her she had to stay home, cook, clean, and be a housewife day in and day out. Frank gave her space. It helped their marriage thrive.

However, Frank had shown Martha how to shoot both the rifle and the shotgun a few times at a range, despite her arguing she did not want any part of it. He told her she must remember there may be a time when she would have to use it. What if a burglar actually broke into the house while he was at work? What would she do then, if she had to defend herself? Frank informed her if she grabbed the shotgun, aimed it at a robber, maybe not even pulling the trigger, the guy would probably think twice before stealing anything in the house or attacking her.

Martha argued the town of Hampshire had never had a history of break-ins. But Frank countered with telling her it could very well happen. And this is what Martha thought was happening now.

She rose up off the bed and walked to the dresser. Another lamp sat there and she tried it. Nothing. Even in the darkness she could make out an old woman of sixty-nine looking back at her in the mirror, whose hair was gray with canals running through the flesh on her face. "Martha, my dear, you're gettin' old," she informed herself, as if the reflection didn't already know.

Her fingers fell on a small brass knob and she pulled, revealing the contents inside of a drawer. The small key to the gun cabinet lay inside. She picked it up, put on her robe and her slippers, and then stepped out into the hall where she heard yet another sound from below.

A shudder ran through her.

The gun cabinet in the hallway had a cherry oak finish. Martha slid the small key into the lock, turned it, and opened one of the two glass doors. She retrieved the Browning, felt its weight, the very thought of having to actually fire it scared her. When she had fired it at the range with Frank by her side showing her exactly how to hold the weapon it damn near knocked her down. She had only fired it three or four times. She really never achieved the knack of shooting it without being able to keep both feet planted in the soil.

Martha checked to see if it was loaded. It wasn't. She slipped two shells out of a box and fed them into the action at the bottom. She stood there, thought for a second, grabbed up a handful of shells and dropped them in her robe's pocket. She had seen her husband do it before, so she thought it had been one of those things someone always did to make sure he or she had enough ammo. But she knew she wasn't going elephant hunting, only trying to find out if someone had truly broken in. Give the guy a little scare while pointing the Browning at him.

With the shotgun tight against her hip, she descended the stairs, one by one, the glow of a light splashed below.

Chapter 17

Something lurked in the kitchen, passing in front of the window, blocking out the moonlight. Barry's eyes registered the top of a head and a white shirt, one in which, in an odd way, gave a soft glow in the dark.

Barry sat up and reached for his bottle and accidently tipped it over. He picked it up as quickly as he could, but after placing it to his lips and tipping it back, found it empty. Only a few small drops had fallen on the floor.

"Who...Wh—Who's there?" Barry's words slurred a bit.

The sound of the flames crackling in the fireplace, throwing shadows on the walls, the only thing heard in the house.

Movement. Slow, as if dragging an object over floor.

"I said, 'WHO'S THERE!'"

A giggle.

"What are you doin'? Tryin' to break into a man's home late at night? Tryin' to catch him off guard?" Barry stood up, staggered over to a lamp on the end table, and pushed the button. When it didn't work, he suddenly remembered the TV had shut off earlier. No power. "Damn!" he spat.

He walked to the front window, gazed out at the silent, nearly pitch black, street. Nothing stirred.

Wait. What moved by the neighbor's Dodge across the street? He thought. Looks kinda like a child. What the hell would they be up this late for? — The wrong door in Barry's mind swung wide — would the child be interested in playing with Uncle Barry tonight? Would the child accept an invitation if he only opened the front d—

As a hand lightly touch his shoulder, Barry jerked back to reality, and spun around to find empty space. His eyes peered into the kitchen, now seeing more heads of figures, more silhouettes. And he heard more than one giggle this time.

"You kids breakin' into a man's home! Trying to be snot-nosed little thieves, are ya?" He sniffed, wiped his nose. "If I see who you are I'm gonna call your parents and have them come after you!"

The figures made no move to come forward, nor did they leave. Their giggles became chuckles. Barry also noticed another white shirt, one with some sort of symbol on it.

"Lookit! Git outta here! Go home!" Barry staggered, almost lost his balance. "Or I'm gonna call the cops!" He made it over to his phone on the end table under a lamp, picked it up, not bothering to place it over his ear and listen to the hollow space where the dial tone used to be, and began dialing.

As soon as he lifted it to his ear a woman's voice spoke. "Hello? What is your emergency?"

"I have bratty kids over her who broke into my house. They won't leave!"

"Kids? Kids are bothering you?"

"Yeah. Tell the men in blue to get over here, now! I want these kids out of my house or...or..."

"Or what Mr. Freckles?"

"Or I'll take matter into my own hands!"

"What kind of matters? They are only children, Mr. Freckles. Not adults. They are not of age yet to be hit."

"Look here! I pay my taxes like anyone else around—" A chuckle sounded from within the kitchen, making Barry spin around.

"I'm sorry? What were you saying, Mr. Freckles?"

"I said I pay my taxes like anyone else in this town and I demand to be rewarded for it!"

"Oh, I see. Well, Mr. Freckles, we can definitely help you. You will be rewarded, I assure you."

"Good."

A long pause. The lady did not speak a word. Barry thought he had lost her. "Ma'am? Are you there?" He spun around, gazing out the front window.

"Yes, I'm here."

"Well? You gonna send the cops?"

"Um, let me see. They may be busy right now."

"Busy?"

"Yeah, something is going on down at the station. I think their phones are down. Mmmm...Let me see. Can you hold on, Mr. Freckles?"

"Sure."

"Thank you." After her words disappeared, Barry stood there keeping the earpiece pressed against his ear, waiting for her voice to return. A thought occurred to him. How the hell did she know his name? Did they tap a person's line whenever they called in for an emergency? No. Couldn't be. Doesn't make sense. They probably monitored the calls, though. Maybe the woman punched it up on the computer or some—

"Mr. Freckles?"

"Yeah."

"So sorry… it seems all of the police are tied up at the moment. I can direct your call over there so you could leave a message."

"Leave a message? This is an emergency lady. I need help!"

"I'm sure you do, sir. But, like I said, the cops are tied up right now. If you wish me to connect you so you can leave a mess—"

"I do not want to leave a message, lady!"

"Now, now, you do not need to raise your voice to me young man."

Young man? He thought.

"I carried you in my womb for nine months before you decided to pop out and make my life a living hell!" The voice changed.

Mom?

"Your no good father couldn't give me the lovin' I needed, so, I had to wait until you were of age, Barry. Couldn't do nothing with that little prick between your legs until it had some growth on it, right?"

"Momma?" he whispered.

A cackle. The voice of his mother vanished, replaced by the operator. "...As I was saying, Mr. Freckles, the cops are all tied up at the moment. If you wish to leave a m—"

"I do not want to leave a message!"

"Mr. Freckles, please don't raise your voice to me. It is not very nice..."

Barry sucked in a deep breath, heard more than one chuckle from his visitors, and then said, "Ma'am, how do you know my name anyway?"

"Why, everyone knows who you are, Mr. Freckles. They know what you've done in the past. They know sometimes you dressed as a clown and lured children away to your house. Didn't you know? People talk, Mr. Freckles. Rumors are started."

Shocked. Barry did not reply. Had the police figured it all out? Were they lying in wait with their rifles and grenades?

"Did you think the Hampshire police do not know of all those horrible things you did to those poor, defenseless, children? They know of your problem, Mr. Freckles. They are aware of those unmarked graves in the woods behind your house...They know of you, Mr. Freckles, a pathetic little man who cannot get it up unless he thinks of a child. Right, Mr. Freckles? Well, I hope you die, Mr. Freckles. I. Hope. You. *Die!* She finished her words with a cackle.

Then, the return of his mother's voice. "Love your mamma, Barry, love her so very much! Love her with all of your hea—"

Barry slammed the receiver down, knocking the phone off the table. Screaming, he threw his bottle across the room into the fire where it shattered. He sunk into his chair, ran a hand over his face, and caught sight of muddy tennis shoes appearing on the floor at the edge of the living room in the glow of the fireplace.

Chapter 18

"A gang of kids?"

"Yes, Gerald, *kids,*" Wendy pressed.

Gerald switched the toothpick from one side of his mouth to the other. "There won't be no gangs comin' in this restaurant!"

"Maybe they want to loot the place since we ain't got any power," Robert said.

"Right!" Gary added.

"It seems so weird for them to stand out there like statues," Wendy said.

A couple of the customers were conversing with each other, not exactly amused the kids were close to their vehicles.

The old guy with the Oldman's Trucking Company hat stood close by. "Have any ideas who those kids are?"

"We don't know at this point. Odd all they're doing is standin' out there."

"Mmmph. Yeah, kinda weird. Hey, by the way, name's Tray." He extended his hand.

"Wendy," she said, introducing herself, taking his hand in hers. "This here is Gerald," she pointed to the cook and to his helpers, "Robert. And Gary."

"Nice to meet ya."

They each shook hands with him and told him the same. Before Wendy could ask where Tray was from, someone shouted, "Hey, look! They're moving toward the window."

Acting as soldiers in a line of battle walking toward the enemy, the headlights illuminated the children, casting them in an eerily glow. The first kid arrived and pressed his face against the front glass, peering directly into a man's face who sat there trying to hold his coffee cup with a shaky hand. Ash-gray flesh stretched over the kid's entire skull, leaving black holes for eyes and a slit for a mouth pocketed with serrated teeth.

The man gasped, fell out of his chair, spilled his coffee, and scrambled back up. "Oh, Lord! That kid is scary-looking!"

More figures filled the view of the window, pressing their faces against the glass, leaving not a mark of condensation from their lips, and placing their palms flat against the pane as if awaiting further instructions.

."Those kids wearing costumes?" Gerald asked.

"I don't know," Wendy said.

"Looks like they're all dressed up for Halloween." Robert said, fumbling for his pack of smokes.

"Must be ready to go trick or treatin'." Gary chuckled.

"I have a bad feeling we're not the trick," Wendy said, feeling the hairs rise up on her arm. A bad feeling coiled inside her gut.

"Say what?" Gerald asked.

"Gerald, I don't like this," Wendy said. "Something isn't right. I don't think they're kids."

Gerald snorted. "They're probably doin' a prank!"

"Ain't never in all my years seen such a thing," Tray said. "Don't believe in monsters, but think I'm seein' them right now."

"What makes you say they're monsters?" Gary asked. "Their wearing costumes, dude. Ain't no such thing as monsters."

Tray looked at the youngster and frowned. "Young man, I think you're wrong."

"They're pullin' a prank, dude!" Robert said.

Gary agreed and they both began walking toward the window.

"Hey, get back here!" Wendy snapped.

The two boys ignored her.

"You know what?" Gerald rubbed his nose, cleared his throat. "I'm gonna take care of this problem once and for all." He slipped into the darkness of the kitchen.

"Where are you going?" Wendy shouted after him, but he didn't reply.

"Ma'am,' Tray said. "I think me 'n you may are on the same page on this. Odd as it is. You feel a chill in the air?"

Wendy agreed. "Something isn't quite right."

Gary and Robert walked directly up to the window. Gary tapped on the glass, right over a boy's nose, and smiled. The dark eyes crawled over him.

"Yo, you tryin' to play some kinda joke or sumthin'? Huh?"

The child blinked.

"Why don't you, and your so-called gang of misfits, go back and play with Barbies and Hot Wheels? Get the hell outta here!" Robert said, walking up and blowing smoke on the glass. "It ain't Trick or Treat night yet, kid."

The kid's the lips stretched into a smile, showing his choppers.

"Think you scare me, dude?" Robert spat. "Why don't you come in here and try it!" He pointed to the floor.

A couple of truckers spoke up, encouraging Robert and Gary. Two others rose out of their chairs; while another guy, tall and stocky rose, pulled out a buck knife and said, "Git outta here kids or Sampson's gonna step up to the plate!"

The faces behind the glass all smiled, displaying their sharp teeth. They turned their heads, acknowledged one another, and giggled.

"You're goin' down, if you step in here!" Gary shouted.

"Go back home to your mommy and daddy, "Robert said, puffing on his cigarette. "Go on back to y—"

"Comin' through!"

Gerald's voice drove people out of the way as he emerged from the kitchen, still dressed in his white apron, waving a pistol in the air, and brushed by Wendy and Tray, giving them both a nasty whiff of grease.

Wendy's eyes widened. Her words of warning for him to stop were drowned out by the cheers of customers as he stepped outside.

Chapter 19

Blood seeped from Dean's nose. He stood, turned his head, and a pain stabbed him in neck. He rubbed it and it receded. "Good God..." He looked at Shro. "Hey, man? You okay?"

Shro slow to rise, held his arm. "Think I broke my arm. Er, maybe not." He amended as he extended and rubbed it.

Eddie gazed down at the two men. He giggled.

"Eddie!" Shro shouted. "What the hell is going on around here?"

"Shro, we need to get out of here and get to the police."

"The police?"

"Scooter's dead. Carolyn's dead."

"Scooter's dead? No way! He was supposed to come and get me. He thought someone had broken into the house."

"Something's not right with your boy up there, I'm telling you. He's changed."

"Changed?"

Eddie started descending the stairs, one by one, gripping the knife.

"What do you mean...changed?" Shro repeated.

"He's not your step-son. He's psychotic. I think he killed Scooter and Carolyn. He wanted to kill me, but I managed to get away from him. He came over to my house and said there was a problem. When I got here, I saw Carolyn. Then Scooter."

"I saw her. Couldn't believe she was dead!"

"I...I never seen anyone dead before, you know?"

"Me neither, but she's gone."

"So, where's Scooter?"

"Upstairs in Eddie's room. Cut open. Eddie used a knife on him."

"Wait." Shro shook his head. He chuckled. "All this can't be right. Eddie must be playin' with us...This whole thing has to be one big joke."

"Joke? The hell it is! You said you saw Carolyn lyin' in her own blood! Scooter is dead, man...Eddie is wacked out of his mind...His face looks different. Not right."

"Say what?" Shro glanced at the stairs and saw Eddie descending. "Stop right there, boy! Who do you think you're foolin'? Get rid of the knife before you hurt someone!" He held onto his sore arm, located his flashlight he dropped and pointed the beam at Eddie. The ash—gray face looked down at him. "Take off the mask, Eddie...Stop all of this nonsense right now!"

"Do you want to play with me, too, Daddy?" Eddie's said. "I want to play some more. I tried to play with Carolyn, but she was no fun. I tried to play with Uncle Scooter, but he wouldn't play fair. Maybe you will Daddy. Will you play fair? No one likes a cheater-cheater-pumpkin-eater."

"Shro, I'm telling you the truth," Dean snapped. "Get your head out of your ass! We need to move...There's evil in this house and it's possessed your boy. Let's go! We can take my car."

"Hold on, man. Hold your water...I'll take care of this. My boy couldn't have killed these people," Shro said. "This is a joke, right? Carolyn," he called, "Get up off the floor...Game's over!"

What the hell is wrong with Shro? He couldn't be that dense! "Shro,

I'm seri—"

"Scooter," he hollered past Eddie. "Come on down and quit this crap!"

Shro can't be this stupid, Dean thought.

"Just 'cause the lights are out doesn't mean it's time to start scarin' people," Shro told Eddie.

"Shro, I'm telling you the truth!" Dean pleaded. "It isn't some game!"

"I'll be the judge of that. I know Eddie loves to play games. He likes those weird comic books. So do you from what he tells me. Probably puts terrible thoughts in his head. Take me for a fool or somthin'?" Shro walked over to the steps and stopped. He glanced back to Dean. "Don't answer that." Then he looked up at Eddie who had stopped descending four steps from his father.

Dried blood covered both of the child's arms. The knife in his hand hung beside his right hip. Eddie's black eyes stared at his stepfather who, now, took a step back. One eye oozed something, trailing down the boy's cheek.

"Eddie? Wh—what the hell's wrong with you, boy?" Shro said in almost a whisper.

"Nothin', daddy. Everything is a—okay. Like you always say." Eddie smiled. Serrated teeth. "I want to play a game with you and Mr. Clemins."

"Eddie," Shro demanded. "Hand me the knife. Right now!"

Eddie's face twitched in the flashlight's beam, the smile under his did not waver. His eyebrows rose, He licked his lips.

Dean could have sworn he saw the boy's skin ripple.

"Boy, give me that knife!" Shro shouted.

Dean backed away. Shro could not be reasoned with.

"Anything for you....*Daddy.* Remember, finders keepers!"

Eddie lunged off the steps, gripping the butcher knife in both hands, dark eyes wide.

Chapter 20

The stairs creaked under Martha's petite frame. Hated the sound, fearing one day she might fall through and end up in the basement. Then she'd probably pay a permanent visit to her Frank. She wasn't ready to die. Not yet, if she could help it.

The thought of her, at her old age, stumbling through the dark, holding a shotgun, tickled her. *What the devil are you doin', Martha? She asked herself and chuckled. What the devil do you think you're gonna do if you actually catch a burglar downstairs? Well, Frank did teach me how to shoot. I'm gonna do it if I have to.*

Halfway down, she smelled apple and cinnamon and noticed three of her scented candles lit on an end table. The flames flickered in front of a picture of a young Frank, taken over thirty years ago.

"Who's there?" she asked, scanning the living room, trying to make out movement. Nothing looked out of place. The recliner sat there, the couch, the television and the bookshelf holding her dolls and her mother's old lamp, the one she received a long time ag–

Wait. There was a missing doll on the shelf. Martha hadn't remembered moving it. All were part of her collection given to her as gifts or if she found them at yard sales, flea markets, or on trips; but the one missing had been one of the two Frank had bought her.

A favorite, wearing a little white dress, little black shoes, and wore pigtails tied up in bright red hair.

Cold air shoved itself through the house. Martha shuddered. "Hello? Who's there? Come out if you don't want to get shot." Martha's voice didn't match her threat she imposed, sounding weak.

Something shattered on the floor downstairs.

What the heck is goin' on in there?

She sucked in a deep breath, continued onward, reached the bottom, and cautiously stepped over to the kitchen and took a peek around the corner. The backdoor hung wide open. The wind had pressed its hand against the door, forbidding it to shut. More cold air shoved its way inside again, fluttering the drapes over the kitchen window. Small refrigerator magnets lay scattered on the floor, along with a shattered dish, the sound she had heard. Overhead, a cabinet door lay open, exposing the cups, glasses and other dishes.

Martha shut the screen and back door, and noticed the side door to the garage open. Had someone taken refuge in her garage? Or was this a trick? Could be. She had seen enough crazy stuff on TV.

Martha laid her hand on the phone on the wall, hoping to hear a dial tone so she could call the police, when the wind snatched the screen door open, slamming it shut.

She stumbled back, dropped the Browning where it clanged on the floor.

"Oh, my!" Martha held a hand over her breast, feeling the quick flutter of her heart. She drew in a long breath, let it out, trying to get herself under control. When she bent down to grab the Browning, she winced.

Damn arthritis…

Rising, holding the shotgun, she heard a giggle.

Martha followed the voice around the corner into the living room where a little girl sat on the floor with her back to her, humming a song Martha didn't quite recognize – though recognized the child.

"Penny?" Martha asked, leaning the shotgun against the kitchen wall.

The child didn't respond, only hummed her tune. Martha figured it out: The Mockingbird Song. She sung it to Penny when she had babysat for the girl's parents.

"Penny? Are you okay?"

"Yeah."

"Why aren't you at home? It's very late for a little girl to be up and not in bed." Martha took three steps and stopped.

"Mommy and Daddy went to sleep."

"I'm sure they have, honey. They have to get up for work tomorrow, bright and early. Did you get up and wander outside, not telling them where you had gone? They'll worry, you know."

"Oh. They won't worry no more." She giggled.

What? Her parents not worry about her? "Penny, now, you know better. Your mom and dad love you very, very much. They always worry of your well—being."

The child giggled.

Martha knew something wasn't right. "Look. Why don't I go and get my coat and I'll walk you back to your house. Sound good?"

"Ohhhh, I don't know. I kinda want to stay and play here."

"Honey, you can't stay here." Martha had taken another step, noticing Penny had something in her hands. She caught a whiff of something foul, covering her nose and mouth. "Sweetie, what do you have in your hands?"

"A dolly."

Martha remembered the missing doll. "Did you take one of my dolls of the shelf?"

"Yeah."

"You know you're not supposed to unless you ask first."

"Mr. Wells said it was okay."

A hand squeezed her gut. "Mr. W-Wells?"

"You know, silly! Your husband."

Martha gasped. "Penny, what are you talking about? Mr. Wells passed away a few years ago. He won't be back."

"Don't count your chickens before they're hatched, Mrs. Wells."

Martha frowned. "Penny! Turn around and look at me. I'm not sure what is going on here. You know better than to walk into someone's home at night and mess with their things. Your parents have taught you better than that."

"They did. They have."

"Well, then, let's get you back home and have a talk with them. I'm sure they're worried."

Penny chuckled. "Nope. Not anymore, Mrs. Wells. They are in a deep, deep sleep. Coma-toasted."

"Penny, let's get you back ho—" Martha placed her hand on Penny's shoulder. The child jerked, twisted around and spread her lips, revealing ivory points, as she gazed through her blackened eye sockets.

Martha stumbled backward.

"Look, Mrs. Wells!" Penny laughed and rose. "See your doll now? I fixed it!" She held the small figure out for Martha to see it. In the glow of the candle light the doll missed a nose and both its eyes. A deep cut stretched across its gut.

"G-Good Lord!" Martha said.

Penny cackled and walked toward Martha, discarding the doll. Lips pulled back in a grin, she gripped a metal letter opener in one hand.

"Wanna play with me?"

Chapter 21

Gerald meant business when he walked through the diner's door holding his head high, holding the pistol down to his side. He loved to watch westerns and always dreamt of being a gunslinger. Time for him to shine. Little did anyone know he kept the gun in the office, locked up in the bottom of his desk drawer. Only he had the key. Not even Jerry knew of the gun's existence. Gerald thought the less the boss knew, the better. He always figured the gun would come in handy one day.

Like now, against a pesky gang of kids.

Before heading out, he picked up a fresh toothpick and slipped it between his lips. Cinnamon flavored, his favorite. He shifted it from left to right with his tongue.

Ain't no gang of kids going to cause trouble here at the diner, he thought. I'll take care of this and be a hero. Maybe my little red headed waitress will see I'm not some goofball. Might arouse her, too, heh-heh, fighting off the kids!

Gerald wasn't a gunslinger by any means, only having shot it at the range less than a handful of times, However, Gerald shoved inexperience away, concentrating on boosting his courage, believing he can use a gun in any kind of bad situations, similar to a full-fledged gunslinger.

Ten children stood apart from each other. Each one of their

heads swiveled in unison, gazed at the cook. All focused on him.

"Play with us, Mr. Gerald?" a little girl in a blue dress, splattered with dried blood, asked. She held out both of her crimson hands. "We'll have some fun, Mr. Gerald!"

"H—how do you know my name, kid?" Gerald asked, shocked. "Are you cut? Where did all of the blood come from?" He also happened to realize most of the kids had blood on their faces and clothes.

"The blood came from the sacrifices...," the little girl responded and the last letter of her word sustained with a hiss. It reminded Gerald of a snake.

"Sacrifices? Wh—what have you kids been doing?"

"It is the..."

"Beginning to..."

"...The end, Mr. Gerald."

Three children spoke, lingering back toward the headlights of the trucks.

"The beginning to...what? Look," Gerald rubbed a hand over his face, "you all need to leave these premises. If not, I'll call the cops!"

"You can't," the girl in the blue dress said. "They won't come." She giggled. So did a few others. "They're sorta in pieces right now."

Gerald stared at her, confused. The pistol became a lead weight in his hand. Suddenly he didn't want to have to point it, much less actually use it on a child. Thoughts of being a gunslinger diminished, replaced with a yellow streak down his back.

One boy, wearing a torn black shirt, shifted away from in front of the headlights and walked toward Gerald with one hand behind his back. "We don't expect all of you to know why this is happening. It. Just. Is. There's nothing you can do to stop it. The hands on the clock are moving, and we, the world, are shifting with it."

Poor Gerald fell more into the land of confusion.

"We know everything about you...and this town. Our master

told us so."

"Master, what the hell you all talkin' about? You all are some kind of gang of delinquents wearin' makeup or masks who don't need to be here! Go back home!" Gerald tried to see if he recognized any of the kids. He didn't.

"There is no going back."

"No return."

Two of the children informed him.

All kids converged on Gerald, closing him in. Three more tore away from the headlights, revealing something very shiny, very sharp in their hands.

The cold air had smacked Gerald in the face when he left the diner, now it seemed frigid. Icy fingers crawled up his spine. And a bitter smell reached his nose.

Shadows of the children fell over the window showing the clientele inside. They were only a step or two from the glass, all peering out at the scene. Although Gerald didn't notice it, Gary and Robert stood behind the window, not believing all of this. They still believed this had been some kind of child's game.

The legs of the children carried them forward, each one holding their own sharp weapon. Smiles flashed over their faces. Dark eyes stared at their prey.

"Stay back!" Gerald shouted. "Stay the hell back!"

"Come now," the little girl in the blue dress said, "don't you want to play with us...?" Again, a long sustaining hiss in her last letter. "It'll be so much fun!"

Gerald backed up, stumbled, almost fell.

"You can't stop it, Mr. Gerald. The beginning to the end is inevitable." the boy in the black shirt said, waving his long blade. "Don't worry. It is much better on the other side in the afterlife."

"Don't make me use this!" Gerald pointed the gun, swinging it back and forth, ready to take aim.

"Don't be such a poopy-head! Come play with us!"

The children all began to cackle. Their blades were raised high, ready to make a change in Gerald's flesh, and the lust for his blood drove the children on. High above in the night air, their master hovered over the scene, circling, admiring his work.

Gerald lifted the pistol, lightly resting his finger on the trigger. The wind picked up and now he could smell the rot in the air coming off of the children. It soured his stomach, making him want to bend over and heave. The ash-gray faces of the children drew closer and closer, their blades at the ready. And they continued to cackle.

His eyelids shut and he prayed to God to forgive him. Even though Gerald knew he had not spoken to God in some time, much less gone to church.

He squeezed the trigger.

Chapter 22

At the sheriff's office, trouble had started hours before. Nancy sat in the dark. She had screwed up. Bad. She had locked herself in a jail cell. Although, she did know those little monsters couldn't get to her.

"Naaaancyyyy? I can smell you by my wittle nose..." the small voice slithered out of the dark, giggling down the hall.

"Go away!" she shouted, holding the broken key, feeling the ridged tip where it had snapped off when she tried to slip it back out of the lock. But she had been in so much of a hurry, slamming the door, trying to jerk the key out after locking herself inside. And the silvery moon, the only companion, accompanying her, shining through the barred window.

"Naaaaaaancyyyyyyyy? Come out come out, wherever you are..."

So much bloodshed had happened in a matter of minutes. So much damn blood! Nancy had never seen anyone bleed so much. Sure, she remembered her daddy's farm when he would wake her up out of bed in the mornings and make her help him with milking the cows, feeding the chickens, and feeding the pigs. Once a week he slaughtered a hog and her father showed her, much to her regret, step by step, how exactly to perform the task.

Her father would take a twenty pound sledge hammer to the poor creature, crushing its skull with not only one blow, but two. To this day, Nancy had always thought in some sick, morbid way her father loved to do it. His face would brighten when he held the sledge hammer and tell her to watch as he murdered the poor creature. Her dad was a good provider and family man, but something would change inside of him when he took to slaughtering.

There were a couple of times when Nancy thought the poor animal had still been alive when daddy sliced it open and the blood and guts fell free from the body, because the carcass would twitch. Daddy assured her the rest of the body dying very slowly.

They say the human body holds ten pints of blood. Nancy figured forty pints had already leaked out on the floor in the office: the sheriff's, both deputies, and the other clerk, May. Poor May." She had never done anything to anybody, always nice and so sweet. She had been Nancy's closest friend. Now, she was no more.

"Come on, Nancy." Play with us …"

"Leave me alone!" Nancy shouted.

"Weeeve meee awohne! Weeve meee awohne!"

"Naaa-na-na-na-naaa-na! You smell like oatmeal and ketchup with worms in it!"

Earlier, before the horror, things were peaceful in the office. Nancy prepared to leave for the night and go home, collecting her belongings. She needed to make some bills out. Especially her house bill, so it wouldn't be late. She had a date too. After four months of sleeping in lonely bed, maybe she'd have some company soon. Perhaps tonight, tomorrow, or the next day.

Carl and Teddy, two of the deputies, were working on paperwork and looked up when a boy ran through the front doors. May gasped. Splattered in fresh blood from head to toe the kid held his hands over his face, muffling his crying.

Teddy hurried over to the boy and asked him what happened.

Was he okay? Where did all of the blood come from? Behind him, Carl rose. Right before he joined his comrade, the boy dropped his hands and his face smeared crimson. He looked up at Teddy, grinned, reached behind his back, pulled out a long knife and plunged it into the Teddy's gut disemboweling him on the spot.

May screamed.

Nancy remembered dropping her purse, covering her mouth with her hand and watching Carl, in shock, backing away.

Efficient and quick, the boy shredded Teddy open in front of them all. Teddy tried to crawl away but the boy was quicker and the tip of his blade found the officer's spine. Teddy's eyes rolled back in his head and he shrieked.

Carl tried to pry the boy off Teddy and the boy twisted around — *God he was quick!* Nancy thought — and opened up in Carl's chest with the blade. He hacked and slashed, plunging it into the man's flesh over and over, slicing open his neck. A long red stream of blood arched in the air, and smacked May in the face.

She continued to scream.

A crimson moat formed around the two fallen deputies while their murderer did not stop, even after they were dead. The boy started mutilating them, cutting off pieces of their face, shearing off their ears, and plucking out their eyes with the blade's tip.

May's voice cracked from all the screaming. Nancy, in shock, tried to get her senses together. She tried pulling her coworker out of the chair. She wouldn't budge.

"Come on! We need to get help, May!" Nancy said.

The boy, finished with the two deputies, stood up, twisted his head toward the women and smiled, showing his sharp teeth.

He blinked his pitch black eyes.

"May! Come on! We gotta go!" Nancy's pleaded.

Two more children — girls, blood-soaked, clothes ripped— stepped through the door.

"Aww shucks! Timmy's havin' all the fun!" one of the little girls said.

The sheriff entered the scene. He had been downstairs locking up a drunk when he heard May scream. "What the hell is going o— holy shit!" His eyes found his deputies, lying in their own bloody muck. His vision shifted to Nancy, watching as she tried pulling May out of her seat.

On impulse, he dropped his hand to his gun. "Nancy? Wh— what the hell's goin' on in here?"

"Those kids, Rich! That boy there," she pointed a finger, "killed Teddy and Carl in cold blood. Look at him! He's wearin' it!"

Rich gazed at her, almost in disbelief, until he saw the child hovering over the corpses, holding his weapon. "Wh—what?" he stammered. "G-Get away from my deputies!"

The boy blinked. "Wanna play, too, Sheriff? These two have grown too cold. Ain't no fun anymore."

Rich drew his gun. "All of you kids don't move!" His mind tried to wrap around the scene, tried to make sense of it. *Small children, killing people? What the hell was going on here? And what was wrong with that child's eyes?* "Hear me? Don't any of you move!"

May sobbed. Nancy gave up tugging on her coworker and stood there, holding May's head against her waist.

"Now, what we are all going to do here is calm down, okay?" Rich said.

Teddy and Carl's killer licked the blood from his lips and grinned at Rich.

Silence fell over the room.

"Nancy? You okay?"

"Do I sound and look okay, Rich? I just saw Teddy and Carl die! How the shit am I supposed to feel? Poor May, here, is in shock."

May's bottom lip trembled. Her mind probed, tried to absorb the horror.

"Sorry, Nancy. Stupid question. Now, look. What I need for you to do," he pointed at the boy with the knife, "is to put the weapon down. "Now."

None of the children moved. Nancy noticed the other two held one hand behind their back.

"Kid," Rich said, "I said put the knife down. Get away from my deputies."

The small murderer obeyed, dropping the blade on the wooden floor. His grin never wavered.

"Move over there by the others."

The boy backed away, keeping an eye on the sheriff.

Rich wiped his face and kept the pistol trained on the kids. "What we are all going to do, kids, is—"

"Are you thinking what I'm thinking?" one of the girls said to the other.

"Mmmmmm, let me see....yeah, I do." the other replied.

"What about you Timmy?"

The boy turned and said, "Yep."

"Hey!" Rich spat. "I'm talkin' to you kids! What we are going to do—"

"Is not a damn thing," Timmy said with a firm tone. "You wouldn't shoot a child, would ya sheriff?"

Could he shoot a child? No, but these weren't normal children! Some abnormally with a sinister demise! Rich thought.

One of the girls started toward him and Nancy saw what the girl hid behind her back.

"She's got a hatchet, Rich!"

"Sheriff?" she asked. "You wouldn't shoot me, wouldja?" Her feet delivered her closer. "You wouldn't shoot a child, wouldja?"

The pistol quivered. "Stay back! Drop the weapon!"

"You would never, ever, shoot a child, wouldja Sheriff?" Nearly a breath away from Rich, the smell of decay reached his nose.

"Stay back!" Rich took a step back.

"Aww! C'mon Sheriff, you don't really want to shoot me, do ya?"

Even though Rich did not drop his gun, the other two rushed forward, overpowering him. The girl slammed the hatchet it into Rich's chest, twisted and pulled it free. She took another stab, sinking it further into his flesh.

The boy picked up his blade and stabbed Rich in the neck. The other little girl held a large fork and she ran the three prongs into Rich's side repeatedly.

The pistol fell from his grip. May screamed again while Nancy began to tug and pull on her again. "Let's go! C'mon, May! We can make it out the back do—"

May jerked, causing Nancy to fall backward into a cabinet and tumble down to the floor. A pain shot through her spine.

May, the good person she had always been, stood up and ran around the desk and tried to pry the children off of the dying sheriff who lay flat on the floor, being mutilated.

It only took a blink of an eye for the girl with the hatchet to turn, swing it, connecting with May's kneecap. The woman dropped to the floor and shrieked, holding her hand over the leaking wound. Her attacker straddled her, hacking away, while bloody bits of poor May sprayed the floor, the walls, the desks, a picture of Rich, Carl and Teddy together sitting erect on the file cabinet sitting in the corner.

Nancy managed to get up and make a run for it. The girl with the fork tore after her, leaving her allies behind to finish off May and the others.

A hallway spread out in front of her. She sprinted as fast as she could. The back door in ahead gave an escape away from this terror.

"Come back, come back, we only want to play with you! We only want to see you bleed!" the girl shouted after her.

"Go to hell!" Nancy twisted her head and shouted.

A cackle rang down the hall. "You first, Nancy Maria!"

How the hell does she know my name? Nancy screamed the thought in her head.

Nancy grabbed and tried yanking the door open. Wouldn't budge. Something blocked it from the outside.

"You can't leave now! The fun's just begun!"

Had the children blocked it? She tried using her shoulder to push it open. It wouldn't give. She twisted around, an instant before seeing three metal points headed for her right eye.

She jerked to the side, out of the way.

The fork bounced off the door and caused the child to stumble backward. Her hollow, leaking eye sockets gazed at Nancy as she ran off, back the same path she had come, darting through the door leading downstairs.

Nancy stumbled, almost lost her balance down the steps leading to the basement. She heard the girl behind her. Rushing into an open cell Nancy shut the door and locked it behind her, failing to get the key free from the lock, shearing it in half.

As Nancy moved away from the bars the girl ran past, glanced over, retreated, stood in front of the cell. She tried to open the door, could not, and Nancy saw anger flutter across the little monster's face.

After a fit of frustration and rage, rattling the cell's door in its frame, the girl calmed down. She smiled. She started laughing. Casually, she walked away, her eyes never leaving Nancy until she disappeared out of sight. Not long after, the lights went out. leaving Nancy in the dark.

Like now.

The voices continued teasing her.

Chapter 23

"**F**inders keepers, Daddy!" Eddie launched off the stairs like a demonic daredevil. If Shro hadn't stepped to the side quick enough, the kitchen knife would have sunk into his chest. Instead, it sliced his arm, through his flannel shirt. He stumbled back, holding a hand over his leaking wound, the flashlight slipping from his grip.

"Eddie! What the hell's wrong with you?"

"You said you wanted the knife, Daddy." Eddie laughed and landed on both feet, facing the two men.

"We need to contact the police, Shro." Dean wanted to get away from all of this, with Scooter and Carolyn dead. Eddie flipping out and changed into something evil. His thoughts shifted to Rachael.

God, I hope she's okay. Where was she? Had her car broke down or what?

"Eddie, stop this! You hurt me!" Shro snapped.

"Don't you want to play, Daddy?" Eddie made a move to go after Shro again with the blade held high over his head, ready to strike.

Dean ran up behind Eddie and grabbed him. "Get some rope or something, Shro!" Eddie thrashed back and forth. The knife left his grip, slid across the floor into the dark. "He's not going to stop!"

"Lemme go! Lemme go!" Eddie thrashed. Dean could taste the stench of decay, almost hurling.

Shro picked up his flashlight and rushed off. Minutes later he returned with a ball of twine. "Don't know if this'll work. It's all I have."

Dean and Shro fought to bind Eddie's hands together while the child convulsed, thrashed. "Tie his feet!" Dean said.

They managed to tie Eddie up while he rolled back and forth, screaming to be released. Shro shot the flashlight's beam over Eddie's face.

Shro gasped. So did Dean.

Eddie's eyes were now hollow. Something black oozed out of the sockets, cascading down both cheeks. His ash-gray flesh had started to peel away. His ivory-colored points for teeth grew.

"What the hell is going on here, Dean? Wh-what the crap is wrong with m'boy?"

"Now do you believe all this?" Dean said. "Huh? Something is *wrong* with him. He killed two people. Almost killed you!"

"Yeah, I believe you," Shro replied. "Uggh! He smells terrible, too, worse than bein' sprayed by a skunk! Do we need to take him to a hospital?"

"Hell, I don't know. I guess it's worth a try."

Together, as they carried Eddie outside while he twisted and fought.

"Hang on. Let me get my SUV," Dean said.

The little shit is strong! Shro thought as he tried to hold onto Eddie.

Dean pulled into Shro's driveway and they stuffed Eddie in the backseat.

"What the frickin' hell is goin' on, Dean?" Shro asked. "What's wrong with Eddie?"

"Man, I do not know." Dean spun the tires and took off down the street. "If we seek some medical attention maybe the doctors will know what—"

"Look out!" Shro pointed at the figures materializing out of the darkness, leaving houses, running across front lawns, armed with butcher knives, cleavers and baseball bats. "Look at those kid! They're coming after us with weapons!"

Children were running down the street and the headlights speared their ash-gray faces.

Dean slammed on his brakes, skidding to a stop. "We need to turn around. We're doomed if we don't." He threw it in reverse and whipped the vehicle around, pointing in the opposite direction, almost clipping the back of a truck. In the rearview mirror, five kids charged the vehicle. "Hold on, Shro!" Dean mashed the accelerator.

Something slammed into the side window where Shro sat, cracking it. He opened his mouth to say, "What the f—" when a tall boy ran close enough to launch a brick at the front windshield, leaving a nasty split in the glass.

Dean drove around a curve and slammed on his brakes. The seatbelts strained against his and Shro's body and Eddie bounced off the back of the front seats.

An old lady with a shotgun stood in the middle of the street.

Chapter 24

Earlier, while Dean and Shro were tumbling down the stairs, Penny threatened to stab Martha with the letter opener. The candle's glow showed her deadly grin. "Play with me, Mrs. Wells. Pretty, pretty, please?"

Martha pressed her back against the end table. "Penny. We need to call your parents. I think we need to get you home."

"Mrs. Wells." She laughed. "I told you they were asleep. They will never, ever, ever wake up again!"

Martha could not make sense of this. Her seventy-year old mind couldn't grasp it. This child's face was ...different, as if the Devil stepped his left hoof into her home.

Penny's smile did not falter as she drew closer, step by step, the letter opener sparkling in the candlelight.

Martha's heart thumped rapidly beneath her breast. Fear wriggled up her spine and ran up the back of her neck. She froze up, knowing she needed to get away from this young, demented child with a lust for her death. But her legs wouldn't respond.

"Mrs. Wells," Penny pouted, sticking out her lower lip, "I only wanna see you bleed. How thin is your blood, Mrs. Wells? Is it thin and watery? Or could it be thick? Have any clots in your legs startin', Mrs. Wells? I'll cure the pressure quick and allow blood to flow freely!"

"Stay away from me, Penny." Martha gripped the end table, feeling the warmth of the candles.

Penny stopped. "Stay away from me, Penny!" She mocked. "Let's see your blood, shall we Mrs. Wells?" She swung the letter opener through the air, inches from front of Martha's gut. "Is it thin? Is it thick?" She giggled.

An aroma of decay filled Martha's nose. Penny's hollow eyes were black pits, oozing something black down both cheeks. She licked her lips.

A large picture of Frank hung on the wall over Martha's doll collection. His frozen smile and his eyes seemed to focus on her. Martha remembered his comfort all those years before his death. *Was she ready to die and join him? Would she give up and allow this child to murder her? Or whatever this...this...thing was? It sure wasn't Penny.*

"Time to die, Mrs. Wells." Penny charged at Martha.

The tip of the letter opener slammed down into the end table, missing Martha as she sidestepped and grabbed a candle and— *God forgive me!* Martha thought —smashed it into the side of Penny's face. Sparks flew, the child fell back, dropped the letter opener, stumbled, and landed on her butt.

Martha scurried around the corner, grabbed the Browning, and lifted the barrel. "Get outta my house, devil!"

Still lying on the floor, Penny's head twisted to the side and glared at Martha. Her lips pulled away from her gums, showing her points. Black ooze continued to drain down both cheeks. Penny's body flipped over on all fours and charged Martha,

"Lord, give me strength and forgive me!" Martha fired the Browning, knocking her back against the counter.

Penny's head exploded. Martha's face and hair caught a crimson spray and brain debris. Her stomach soured.

The girl's body did not stop the attack.

Headless, the Penny-thing charged.

Martha shrieked and moved to the side. The Penny-thing hit the lower cabinet, bouncing back, leaving a goo of Penny blood.

Martha pulled the trigger, this time blowing the Penny-thing's arm off. It spun around, a fountain of blood sprayed from the stump, creating abstract, crimson marks on the room. Its remaining arm flailed while one leg lifted off the floor and the other balanced on the ball of its foot, accomplishing a macabre ballet until it bounced off a wall.

Still, the headless body did not stop.

It rocketed after the old woman.

Martha escaped out of the backdoor while her knees popped while Arthur gave her hell for it. She hurried across her front lawn and into the middle of the street only to see a vehicle barreling down on her.

Behind her, Penny's semi-armless and headless body pursued.

Chapter 25

The figure wearing the muddy tennis shoes stepped into Barry's living room. He wore filthy jeans and a shirt caked with mud. The shirt displayed a symbol behind the dirt, a skull and crossbones with the words PETERSON ELEMENTARY written over it. The indention in the boy's head matched where Barry's shovel had hit him. The kid's flesh stretched over his skull had long but decayed. Bits and pieces flaked the floor. Empty eyes sockets held darkness.

The boy's head tipped to the side, then to the other, standing there quietly, staring at Barry.

Barry saw the symbol and remembered the day when he had abducted the child, not very many years ago...

...The spring breeze blew and Barry could smell a musty fragrance carried with it: strong perfume from someone who had perhaps passed by and gone inside. His face screwed up in its disgust. The parking lot at the apartments where he parked had been nearly been empty except for a few cars. The apartments themselves looked Section—8. Barry figured them to be roach motels. Nasty places to live with holes in the walls and low income welfare checks in the mailbox. He couldn't imagine living in the muck.

The faster he collected his treasure, the faster he could leave.

He opened the car's door and stepped out. Used syringes lay on the pavement. Dried blood filled inside one of them. A pile of discarded broken beer bottles butted up against the curb.

Barry took in the full sight of the apartments, scanning for anyone who might be outside on the balconies. He didn't see a soul. He grinned and headed toward the playground.

Two children played on the merry-go-round. One swung on the swing set, seeing how high he could get without flipping over the bar before falling out on the ground. The two chains holding the vinyl seat hugged the boy's bottom while attempted to swing higher and higher. A young woman walked into the picture and Barry stopped in his tracks. She grabbed the child on the merry-go-round and dragged him off, cursing. From what Barry could tell, the woman was pretty pissed at her kid.

Barry had thought he would have had to choose between the two kids.

Now the choice was made.

The boy swung higher and higher as Barry stepped forward, nearing the playground. He looked back, watching as the woman dropped out of sight with her kid through a hallway door.

He directed his attention to the kid.

"Hello there," Barry smiled.

The kid swung back and forth, eyed him, saying not a word.

"Hello," he said again. "How are you, young man?"

"I'm not 'spose to talk to strangers," the boy replied, slowing his swinging.

"Well, I'm not a stranger. I'm your Uncle Barry."

"I don't have an Uncle Barry."

Barry grinned. "You do now. You know why you have an Uncle Barry?"

The boy paused, slowing his swinging to a stop. "Why?"

"Because your uncle has brought you something really cool."

The boy frowned. "Like what?"

Barry reached into his pocket and pulled out a plastic egg. Clear on one side, blue on the other. Inside the clear side was a miniature toy airplane. With his thumb and forefinger, Barry held the prize closer so the boy could see it better.

His little blue eyes lit up. His butt slid off the swing and he wiped a dirty hand over his Peterson Elementary shirt. "Wow!"

"Do you want it?"

"Sure! Can I really have it, mister?"

"Why, you sure can! Here." He held out his hand, where the egg rested in his palm.

The boy went to Barry.

Barry looked both ways, behind him, and back to face the kid. A tingle of nervousness ran through his body, a shudder of both fear and excitement.

The boy grabbed the egg and gazed at it.

"You know," Barry said, looking at the child only a foot away from him, "I have a whole box full of those in my car. Do you want another one?"

The child tried unscrewing the egg, but couldn't.

"Here. Let me open it for you." Barry opened it, gave both halves back, and watched as the boy's face lit up even more.

With his small fingers the boy scooped out the airplane and said "*Vroom!*" flying it back and forth through the air. "Cool!"

"There's more where *that* came from, kid." Barry stuck a thumb over his shoulder.

"I want another one."

"Swell. Wanna hold my hand? We don't want you to get hit in the parking lot, do we?"

"Nope, Momma always told me not to cross the street unless I was holdin' an adult's hand."

"Sounds like she's a good mother."

"Well, I guess. She's not home right now. Gone to the grocery."

"She left you at home by yourself?"

"Yep."

Barry's spirit soared. It had been such an easy kidnapping, no mother around, no wondering eyes. At least there hadn't been, so far.

The kidnapper and child walked to the car and when the car's door opened, Barry gave the boy two more plastic eggs and explained the he had forgotten – Silly him – the rest. They were back home. He talked the child into accompanying him for an ice cream cone. The child gladly accepted the invitation...

..."Uncle Barry," a hoarse voice came from the small figure standing over Barry. "Got anymore plastic eggs with candy on one side; toys on the other?"

The smell of dirt and rotten flesh covered Barry's face. He sat there speechless.

The child turned toward the kitchen and something fell out the back of his skull, hit the floor, and squirmed. "Come on over. Uncle Barry is going to give us some toys and candy." He looked at Barry. "Aren't you, Uncle?"

Barry swallowed. Could he be dreaming again?

He heard a drawer in the kitchen pull out, shut. Three more figures entered into the living room. All were filthy from the soil they crawled through to reach the surface. All wore shrouds of decay and what clothes hadn't yet rotted away.

"There may be more on the way, Uncle Barry," one of the dead children said and chuckled. "Got enough toys to go around, Uncle?"

Barry's bottom lip quivered.

Chapter 26

Wendy, Tray, Robert, Gary, and the small group of people under the roof of Sam's Truck Stop watched as Gerald conversed with the kids. They saw the kids speaking to him and saw the changing expressions filter over his face. Before long, as the young group converged on the cook, people gasped when the sharp weapons were revealed.

"We've gotta do something!" Wendy said.

"Anyone have any kinda weapon in here we can use?" Tray asked.

"I don't know. Maybe we can find something in the back. A broom handle or somethi—"

"Look! The cook is raising his pistol! He's gonna shoot one of them!" a customer hollered.

"Oh no!" Wendy didn't want to see a child die, even though these kids wanted to start trouble. There was no reason to shoot a child in cold blood. Gerald needed to try a different approach, or something.

"Holy sh—" a voice rang as they saw Gerald pull the trigger and shoot the closest child to him. The small fragile skull blew apart, spraying the front window with blood and something dark and oozing.

Robert and Gary took a step back when it happened. There had only been an inch of glass between them and the slaughter. They shielded their face as if the gruesome spray would have hit them.

Wendy gasped, held her hand over her mouth.

Tray's mouth hung open, unable to squeak out a word.

The rest of the customers followed in the wake, appalled. And now, as if an additive to the horror, they saw something making the scene worsen: the headless body rose up and from the meaty stump where the head used to rest, a geyser of blood shot out.

It took off and ran full throttle at the cook, who had no time to react because his eyes opened right after firing the bullet.

The cook's body slammed the ground.

The rest of the little monsters attacked Gerald, stabbing him, laughing as they began their murder. Gerald did not go down without a fight. He rose up screaming, wounds in his chest leaking, and shoved small bodies away. They stumbled, falling over like dominoes.

Gerald searched for the gun.

Nowhere to be found.

Scrambling toward the front door, Gerald slipped and hit the window face-first and bounced off, smearing his blood on the pane.

The children who had been shoved away returned. All piled on top of Gerald, slicing more of his flesh open. With a throat-full of blood, Gerald gasped for air. He slapped a bloody palm on the window and a mournful squeak accompanied his hand's bloody descent on the window as his body expired.

Silence filled the air in the diner. Shocked faces, each rooted themselves to the floor, not moving, not knowing what to do or what to expect.

Until the children's attention shifted to the diner's front door.

Their dark eyes glared. They smiled, showing their points, observing the people inside. Slowly, with Gerald's blood dripping off their bodies, they stepped toward the door. The headless one joined them holding a large blade.

"W-We need to do something!" Wendy knew her words were weak. But people did turn their heads and look at her. Everyone acted as a statue. No one knew what to do. Then she added: "Let's block the door!"

Wendy scrambled over to the front doors. Her fingers barely brushed the metal handle when it wrenched open, allowing the cold air to blow in. Wendy grabbed hold, yanked it shut, and came face to face with an ash-gray colored child looking at her through the glass, licking its lips.

Three more kids joined the other and gave the door a yank.

"A little more help over here somebody!" Wendy called out.

Three truckers skidded to a stop behind her and had barely grasped the handle before it jerked opened again.

"What the hell is this? They're only youngin's!" one of the truckers said. "My little boy ain't this strong!"

"They ain't kids. They're monsters!" Wendy informed him.

A close up look appearing through the glass showed the guy the truth. He gasped. Obviously, the guy was a few pages behind the situation.

The headless one grabbed the door, helping his friends, and Wendy could see inside of his bloody stump. Her stomach rolled and soured. And the more her vision peered into it, the more she wanted to tear it away.

Two eyes blinked beneath a transparent wet film.

"J-Jesus ..." Wendy's eyes widened.

Two claws jutted out, gripping the edge of the bloody flesh, and folded away the skin. At one time a child, happy, outgoing, who loved to ride his bike through the trails and play baseball had been replaced: Peeling off the remainder of the flesh a huge rat stood upright in a pool of black blood.

Wendy screamed until her voice cracked.

She fainted.

Chapter 27

"Holy —"

"Shit!"

The SUV's tires slid, causing the vehicle to jerk sideways, almost taking out the fragile old woman with her face twisted in fear. Shro and Dean's stomachs tightened up. In the backseat, Eddie thrashed back and forth, using his tied up legs and feet to thump the back of Shro's seat.

"Let me go!" Eddie shouted.

"No!" Shro said, turning around. "Calm down!"

"Hey, Shro? Look! What is that?" Dean pointed.

The headlights captured a figure running on three legs, and, at first, Shro pegged it as a dog. Further observation showed him it not being a canine, something sinister. Shro opened his mouth trying to speak a word, stammered a few letters, delivering nothing off his tongue.

"Help me! Please?" the old woman startled Dean. She shrieked. "Help me!" Spittle flew from her mouth, spraying the glass. Blood splattered across her face.

No sooner than when Dean opened his door and the woman stepped back, he heard Shro actually muster out a word — a word of warning— before the old woman's body jammed against the door and it shut back.

Dean's fingers were nearly chopped off.

The three-legged thing had jumped on the lady and had taken her down to the pavement. The shotgun slipped out of her grip, the barrel's tip hit the pavement first, and it bounced twice before skidding off to the side.

Dean looked at Shro. "Get the gun! I'm goin' save that lady!"

"I don't know, man I ain't goin' out th—" Shro's word shaved off as Dean slid outside, leaving the driver's side door wide open.

"Let me go! Let me go! Let me GO!" Eddie continued. The flesh around his wrists had started to peel under the stretch of the twine, revealing lines of black.

Dean pried the figure off of the lady and threw it off to the side. It quickly rose back up. Dean's jaw dropped. The creature was headless, missing an arm, and wearing a little girl's nightgown.

Dean had no time to react when it attacked him, knocking the wind out of him. If there had been a head, the stump wouldn't have leaked so much blood on Dean's face. He struggled, rolling and tumbling on the pavement. The small hand of the headless creature wrapped around Dean's throat and squeezed.

Shro saw the old woman stand and stumble over to the shotgun. Through all of this, the rearview mirror had swiveled in his direction and he witnessed figures had appearing out of the darkness, as if it were magic, or an illusion gone completely insane. First there were silhouettes, then they formed into those devil children.

"Whoa!" Shro unclicked his seatbelt and grabbed Dean's door to pull it shut.

Eddie's hands pulled Shro back and clamped down on his ear using his razor-sharp teeth.

A warmth spilled down his face and he shrieked.

The old woman picked up the firearm and yelled at Dean to try and get away from the beast if he could. Somehow he managed to bring both knees up into the gut of the headless figure and pushing back, sent the thing sprawling. Coughing from the choke hold the creature had given him, a deafening blast rang out, blowing the figure in two.

Dean rose and saw both halves twitching, leaking black blood. "Jesus ..."

The old woman stepped over, held out a hand to help Dean up, which he surely took. "Thanks," he told her.

"You're very welcome, young man."

Dean heard Shro shriek and saw Eddie's mouth stretching Shro's ear away from the side of his head. He sprinted to his vehicle and wrenched open the back passenger door and grabbed Eddie.

"Get this kid off me!" Shro cried. "Damn it hurts!" Eddie's hand lay over Shro's eyes while the other clawed at his throat and his teeth sunk into Shro's ear.

Dean had to actually pry Eddie's mouth off Shro using his fingers, making damn sure the child's teeth didn't take them off. Eddie thrashed as Dean dragged him away from the vehicle.

Shro held onto his wound, moaning.

Dean struggled with Eddie and noticed a horde of children running down the street, all holding sharp weapons.

Eddie became too much and broke free from Dean. The boy ran off into the darkness, which seemed to consume his small body.

"C'mon!" Dean shouted at Martha and headed to the SUV.

The lady slid into the back and Dean shifted the transmission into drive and mashed own on the accelerator, leaving a long skid mark on the street as they took off. Behind them the children took chase until they knew they could not keep up.

The SUV took a curve, slid, and they passed more houses.

On the lawns they saw the dead who had been dragged out of the homes and laid out, as if they were on a cooling board. Victims of the slaughter, who were all adults with a few of the children standing over them, blood dripping from either their blades or metal scissors. Their eyes watched the SUV pass by, their sadistic glares focused on the ones who continued to live.

"What the hell is going on here? Does anyone have a clue?" Dean spoke, after a small brief of silence. "You doin' okay over there, Shro?"

Shro only grumbled, holding his wound. "Not *a*—okay. But I'll manage. My arm stopped bleedin'."

""I think your ear has, too." Dean adjusted the rearview mirror. "How about you, ma'am? You hurt?"

"No. I'm fine, thanks," she replied. "I don't know what's going on around here. It's as if every child in town decided to be mass murderers."

"I have no clue why this is happening. I am at a total loss."

"Thank you for stopping and saving me."

"No, I should thank *you* for saving *me*…umm?"

"Martha."

"Martha. I'm Dean. This is Shro."

Shro held up his hand, said "Hello," returned it to his aching ear.

"Nice to meet you both. Wish it would have been under normal circumstances."

"I agree," Dean replied.

Martha bit her bottom lip. "That creature I killed used to be a little girl named Penny." Her eyes watered. "She use to…use to come down and play with my dolls. I've babysat her since she was old enough to walk. Now, I…I can't believe it. She came at me with my letter opener and," she wiped her eyes, "and tried to stab me."

"The boy who got away from us, it was Shro's stepson. He murdered a girl named Carolyn and a guy named Scooter."

"Carolyn?"

"Yeah."

"Oh, Lord! Her and her parents go to the same church I go to. I remember when she was little. Such a cute child."

"I knew her, too. Nice girl."

Driving out of the suburb, they pulled onto the main road. "We need to get you medical attention, Shro," Dean said.

"Okay." Shro's arm and what was left of his ear pained.

"We'll head to the hospital. I wonder if Rachael is there, working over since the power is down."

"You haven't talked to her?" Shro asked.

"Not since earlier." Dean still worried something bad had happened to her. She should have been home way over an hour ago, but he knew sometimes she had to work over. If so, with the phone towers down, she wouldn't have been able to reach Dean to tell him anyway.

"I haven't heard from Wendy. Hope she's okay. Do you think the hospital will have power?" Shro asked.

"They should have a backup generator."

"Let's pray everything is normal there," Martha said. "If not, it's not going to be pretty."

Dean shuddered at thoughts of children running the hospital halls holding scalpels, killing patients.

"Do either of you read the Bible?" Martha asked.

"I have," Dean said, "but not much. How 'bout you Shro?"

"Some," Shro said.

"Why do you ask?" Dean said.

"Because I've read a lot of it. I have an odd feeling. I'm not sure if I should say or not. But we may very well be in the book of Revelations. Don't ask me why, it feels...different."

"Why would you think that?"

"Because it seems, so far, the world has suddenly turned upside down. Children murdering people is unheard of. Look, we don't have any power and the air feels different. It's ... stale and cold."

"I agree with you. It's as if evil has settled over this town."

"What, you mean the end of the world?" Shro asked.

"Yes," Martha responded, "in a rather odd way. You know the

Devil has a weird way of doing evil."

"Like he has some, sick sense of humor?" Shro frowned.

"Yes. God wouldn't do this."

"What do you think he'd do? Send a flood and wipe out everyone? Have someone be Noah and build an ark?" Shro chuckled.

"It's possible," Martha explained. "I cannot see God sending these creatures, once innocent children, to kill people."

"I agree," Dean said. "I believe God would wipe out the entire world in one smack."

Shro thought for a minute. "Like *Smackdown*? You know, wrestling on TV?"

Dean frowned. "No. I'm talking about the power He has. Remember, he placed man into this world. He can take him out."

"You're right," Martha said.

"You have to be kiddin'?" Shro said, shaking his head. "Maybe all of these kids woke up one morning and ate the wrong cereal or somthin'. Got somethin' in their blood."

"Are you for real, Shro?" Dean snapped. "You've already witnessed people dying, headless children running around, Eddie attacking you, biting your ear off, and you're going to sit over there and *not* believe it?"

"Well, I didn't say I totally don't believe, but I may have questions."

"Such as ..?"

"Well, let me think...hmm. Maybe I don't."

"You don't because you're feeling the fear Martha and I are feeling. Wake up, man. Open your mind. Something is up. What about Wendy? When did you speak to her last?"

Shro's stomach knotted up. "We need to go check on her! I spoke to her earlier, about six. She's workin' tonight."

"Okay. Look." Dean wiped a hand over his face. "The hospital isn't far. I'll park and run in and check on Rachael. She can get your ear fixed up. Then we'll head to the truck stop. Cool with you?"

"Sure, man. You have a rag or something I can hold over my ear? My hand is wet with blood."

Dean looked in the rearview mirror. "Martha, would you see if there's a rag or something back there Shro can use?"

"Sure," Martha replied.

The SUV drove east, passing an old Chevy station wagon off on the shoulder holding the remains of two adults and two missing children.

Shro, Dean, and Martha took no notice to it, thinking it had only been a broken down vehicle.

Chapter 28

Voices pulled Wendy from her slumber. Her eyes opened and Tray's face appeared.

"You okay? You took a nasty fall. Me and one guy picked ya up and placed you here on the floor."

She winced, rubbed the back of her head.

"You hit your head when you fainted."

"I did?"

"Here, take my hand," Tray told her, grinning. "Up ya go!"

Wendy grabbed his hand and stood up. The room spun. She tried shoving back the dizziness, absorbing the views in the room.

The front windows were intact. Not shattered or broken. The truck's headlights still blazed and Gerald's bloody hand print had dried up, left there, indicating the last mark of the cook before his demise. The children all lined up as if in a firing line, eight to ten feet away from the glass, staring intently into the diner at the ones who still lived.

Wendy did not see the rat.

Tables were piled in front of the doors, stacked high, along with chairs. Truckers sat talking to one another, pausing when they saw Wendy, forcing a smile, then resumed their conversation. They looked worn out. Some drank cold coffee and one sat off to himself eating a chocolate bar.

"Tray? Tell me what happened after I fainted," Wendy asked.

"Here, have a sit first." He pulled over two chairs and sat beside her. "After you fainted one of the guys picked you up and got you out of harm's way. Couple of those kids—or what the shit they are called now, monsters, whatever now—grabbed hold of the front door and pulled with all their might. Two slipped in, including the monster that came out of the kid's body. Both started grabbing people and shoving them outside. Damn, they were quick! Once the victims were outside…." He shook his head.

"They were killed."

"Yes, ma'am."

"You said the rat was inside the diner?"

"Yes, ma'am. It was a huge one. Stank somthin' rotten. One of the last men it snatched it dragged him outside and gnawed his face off."

Wendy cringed, glanced outside. The memory of the large rat crawling out of the child's skin gave Wendy a recollection of the horror. She shuddered, thinking of those eyes staring out of the stump where the head used to rest.

"Nope. Not pretty. I think it was Robert who was grabbed by the rat. In the madness of the attack, the last I saw him do was trying to keep the door shut. I haven't seen him since."

"Damn." Wendy closed her eyes.

"Never saw nothin' like it. Saw a bear attack a buddy of mine when I was younger; barely made it away from the beast. Poor guy lost his arm from the elbow down. But this huge rat? Different story. Damn thing dug into the guy and didn't stop. The creature didn't want to leave anything behind. None of us could save him, either. One of his buddies—Gary I think—and two other guys tried to be a hero and ran outside to save Robert. They didn't make it back in."

Wendy's stomach soured. "What of the kid who got inside?"

"Huh?"

"You said there were a two. A kid and the rat."

"Oh, sorry, we have the delinquent back in the storage room, tied up."

"The storage room?"

"Yeah. He's a feisty one', but we've managed to hold him back there. Took four of us to do it."

"Why did you keep one of them? Why not beat it back outside or kill it?"

"Well…right before Gary tried saving his buddy, he mentioned the kid looked like yours. Do you have a child named Eddie?"

Wendy's face drained of blood. *Eddie? Here? One of those...those monsters?*

"Hey, you aren't looking so good. Gonna faint on me again?" Tray held onto her, afraid she would fall and land on the floor. "Wendy? Don't faint. Stay with me, honey."

Wendy didn't faint and her dizziness had subsided, but her stomach rolled and her head pounded something fierce. "Tray?"

"Yeah?"

"Can you look over behind the counter and see if there's a bottle of Tylenol? I need to get rid of this pain in my head."

"You gonna be okay sitting there?"

"I'm fine."

"Hang on." He stepped behind the counter, searched for the bottle, not having much luck. "Stay right there. I'm goin' see if someone has some."

"Thanks." Wendy closed her eyes and cradled her head in her hands. *Eddie? One of those creatures? What the hell is really going on? The power goes out and suddenly those demonic kids show up and start killing people?*

"Gonna be okay, there?" a deep voice said.

Wendy opened her eyes and looked up at a black guy in bib overalls. He frowned. "Ma'am? You gonna be okay?"

She forced a smile. "I'll be okay. Thanks."

"I overheard Tray telling about your boy. I wanted to let you know I helped put your boy back there."

"He couldn't possibly be like those kids out there, right? Please tell me it isn't so."

A sad look flashed across the man's face. ""Fraid so. Stings a bit, but it's the truth. He tried to cut me before I got the knife away from him. He cut Mack pretty deep." He pointed to a guy who held his arm wrapped up in a white bandage. "I think he'll need stitches. Cut all the way to the bone."

Wendy tried to take all of this in. A nightmare. *How could her Eddie possibly be one of those monsters?*

"Here ya go. One of the guys had some." Tray walked up with a Coke and two Tylenol and handed them to Wendy. She knocked back the pills and took a long drink of soda. She hadn't realized her mouth had been so dry.

"Thank you very much, Tray."

"No problem. I see you've met Thomas."

"Well, we haven't formally," Thomas said. "But nice to meet you Wendy." He held out his large hand. Wendy shook it.

"Guys, I want to see Eddie," Wendy said.

Tray and Thomas exchanged a glance. "Sure," Tray said. "We'll go with you. You need to be very cautious. 'kay?"

"Cautious?"

"He's not exactly a happy camper. He's one of those monsters. We tied him to a chair, and not so sure if it'll hold 'em," Thomas warned.

Wendy blinked. A bad feeling coiled inside her gut.

"Please, just be cautious of Eddie, Wendy," Tray said.

"I will." Wendy stood up. The room shifted and she grabbed the back of the chair, preventing herself from falling. Tray and Thomas grabbed her. "Thanks, guys."

When Wendy could stand without assistance, she followed Tray and Thomas as they led her into the dark of the kitchen, shoving it away with their flashlight beams.

Behind the door to the storage room, Wendy could here Eddie giggling.

Chapter 29

Shro sat in the passenger seat holding a rag over his aching ear. Shro still had trouble swallowing all of this terror. This kind of thing only happens in movies or television shows. *What would the Duke boys do in Hazard if something like this happened? Would they and Uncle Jesse be armed with shotguns, driving the General Lee over the fields and shooting these zombie-like children? And would they have the string on their bow pulled back and the tips of their arrows lit with fire at the ready to shoot the kids, blowing them apart? Now there's something to think about…*

"What?"

"I said are you doing okay over there, Shro?" Dean asked. "How's your ear?"

"Hurts like a bitch. I think it's stopped bleeding."

"Has your arm stopped bleeding?"

"Yeah. Hurts too."

"I bet. We'll get you to the hospital soon. Rachael will be able to take care of your wounds."

Shro began to say something else when Rachael's Honda came in view.

"There's my wife's car!" Dean pointed. Fear gripped him. *What was her car doing way out here and not at the hospital?*

When Dean pulled the SUV in front of the Honda, something rolled against the back of his feet. Reaching down, he grabbed a flashlight. "Looks like we have two flashlights now. Didn't even know I had one in here." Dean had to shake and smack the side of the flashlight to work. He couldn't remember when he had replaced the batteries last. "This would have helped, earlier, when I first tracked through your place, Shro."

Shro nodded. "Having two are definitely better than only one."

Martha and Shro slipped out of the SUV.

"Yep," Dean cupped his hands around his eyes and peeked inside the Honda's window. No Rachael. He opened the door and saw her purse on the passenger seat and the keys in the ignition. *Where the hell could she be?* The thought of her trying to flag someone down in a car or truck and being kidnapped horrified Dean. *No,* he told himself, *don't think like that. She is a strong woman. She wouldn't let herself fall into a bad situation— would she?*

Martha and Shro walked over to Dean.

"No. This doesn't sit right. Something must have happened to her."

"Dean, don't jump to conclusions, hon," Martha assured. "She may be okay. She might have broken down and walked off, trying to find a house to see if she could get a ride. You never know."

What Martha said could be possible. If Rachel had tried to use her cell phone and found no signal, she might try and find someone's house out here. Though, he couldn't remember if he had ever seen any other houses out this way. And when Dean began to feel slightly better, the hole opened, and he fell.

"Hey, look over here!" Shro shot the beam of his flashlight. "Its blood. There's a trail of it. Guess something got hit by a car and crawled into the woods to die."

Martha frowned. "That's not what Dean wanted to hear, Shro."

"Oh, sorry," Shro said. "I figured it was an animal, not a person."

"It may very well be," Martha replied.

"Right now, anything is possible with those children or creatures or whatever it is running around killing people," Dean said. "I'm gonna investigate. You two can stay if you want. I'm going into those woods."

"I don't think my legs will be much use tracking through the woods at night. If I was thirty years younger, I'd take you up on it. Shro? Can you go with him?"

"Er, yeah. I'll go with ya ...I guess," Shro's said, "taking the blood soaked rag away from his ear." He didn't say it, but he really didn't want to go. When he saw Dean looking at him, he changed his tone: "Ain't 'fraid of nothing, Dean. I'm good to go with you."

Even to him his response was weak.

Dean frowned. Not so sure about Shro. Now he knew why he hardly spoke to him. The guy was a goof. "Martha, we'll be back as soon as we can. If you want, sit in the Honda or in the SUV until we return."

"Sounds good." She waved goodbye to the men. "You want my shotgun? Just in case?"

Dean paused. "Good idea." He hurried to the SUV, grabbed the firearm.

"You may need these, too." Martha pulled out six shells from the pocket of her robe. Dean grinned. "Thanks."

"Know how to load it?" Martha asked.

Dean blinked. "Not really."

"Here, I'll show you." Martha gave Dean a two minute crash course on how to load it and flick the safety off. "Never shot a gun before?"

"Once or twice when I was a kid."

"You'll be fine, Dean. Please be careful."

"I will. How'd you learn to shoot?"

"My husband Frank. He showed me a long time ago. He passed away a while back."

"I'm sorry."

"Thank you. Good man, my Frank." A tear slid down Martha's cheek.

"Hey, um, aren't you cold? There's a jacket in the back of the SUV if you need it."

"Thanks. I think I'll grab it. This robe isn't very warm."

"We should be right back."

"Be careful."

"We'll try."

Dean and Shro slipped into the woods. Their flashlight beams cut away the dark, allowing the two to follow a red trail. Dean's gut tightened at the sight of seeing more blood.

"Could still be from an animal."

"Let's hope. But where's the carcass?"

"A wild dog or a wolf could have dragged it off."

"True." Thoughts of Rachael helpless, bleeding, maybe attacked by a wolf did not set well for Dean's. *Perhaps Shro was right, it could be dead animal. But it did not explain Rachael's disappearance.*

"Awful quiet here, Shro. Not a good sign."

Shro agreed.

Pressing on, they followed the trail leading into a clearing. A figure sat in the center, impaled into the ground. The men's first thought had been a scarecrow. A good assumption, until the flashlight's beam splashed over Rachael's corpse.

Dean screamed. He fell down on his knees, dropping the shotgun and flashlight.

Shro gasped.

And neither Shro nor Dean noticed the small forms materialize out of the darkness.

Chapter 30

"Momma? That you? Wanna play with me?"

In Tray's beam of his flashlight Wendy saw her son. She held her hand over her mouth, trying not to puke from the malodorous smell of decay.

"Momma? Those bad men put me in this chair." He stuck out his bottom lip. "One of them slapped me. They need to be punished."

Wendy glanced at the two men. Thomas hung his head. "He cut Mack. I think I already told ya. Before we contained him and tied him up."

Wendy nodded. "You did. It's …okay." She didn't know if she approved or disapproved. She looked at her son. "Eddie? Why are you doing this?"

Eddie grinned. "It's the beginning of a new chapter in the world. Can't stop it. No one can. The hands of time are moving. We, the world, are shifting forward. Might as well face facts, Mom, and give up your blood."

"What are you talking about?"

"The end, Momma. The end of the world. Everything must die. All life must die so darkness can live. There is no turning back. No return."

"The end of the world?"

"Yup." Eddie laughed and when he spoke again a chorus of four different harmonized as one: "We don't expect you mortals to understand, Wendy. We expect you mortals to allow us to watch you bleed. All you pathetic humans who have given Earth nothing but pain and despair have successfully destroyed a world given by your maker. A beautiful world, it was. Wars. Depression. Corruption. Lies. Sin. You mortals gut each other like the monsters you are. You humans can't feel pain because of all the scar tissue you've caused.

"Those two distasteful, horrid mortals," the voices spat, "should have never been allowed to leave the Garden of Eden for the pain they caused. God should have crushed them, forbidding them to replicate. But no! He let your race continue. And then his son, crucified, purged himself for your sins.

"We despise you creatures! Every one of you shall die!" The cords in Eddie's neck stood out and spittle flew from his lips as the voices spat: "Die and squirm in your own blood while the maggots consume your dead flesh, feasting on the defunct brain you carry inside your skulls!"

A chill squirmed down Wendy's spine. "Eddie, stop it!"

Tray and Thomas winced at this evil.

"Sorry, Mommy, can't control what is going on inside of me..." Eddie's voice pleaded. Beads of sweat ran down his face. "Help me..."

Wendy started to go to her son.

"No!" Thomas' words were drowned out when Eddie began thrashing back and forth in the chair.

Wendy stopped.

The twine strained over Eddie's body, cutting into the kid's arms. Screaming, each orifice on his face – mouth, eyes, ears – became black holes. Bugs clawed their way out of each one, covering the boy's frame, creating a shimmering film of insect. It rasped: "Let me go! Let. Me. Go!"

Wendy backed into Tray. She glanced over her shoulder, eyes wide. Both men could only stare at the morphing creature tied to the chair.

The Eddie-thing thrashed, causing the twine to break apart. The bugs used their claws to stretch open holes which had been Eddie's eyes and mouth. "You'll be sorry, mortals!" Guttural laughter filled the room.

Unlike the headless creature Wendy witnessed earlier, this one took on a different approach. Its face split down the middle and the folds of insect film peeled back, revealing a transparent, glistening cocoon layered with pulsating varicose veins. A snout shoved through the film. The face of a huge rat stared at the mortals in the room.

Claws cut through the boy's fingers, popping each fingernail onto the floor, freeing themselves from their binding, as well as ripping away the legs and feet. The mutilated cadaver of Eddie fell back on the chair, a startling finish, with only a thin piece of flesh.

The rat slid off the chair, opened his arms, smiled. "Tah—*dah*! How do ya like me now, Mommy?"

Tray grabbed Wendy and dragged them both from the room. Thomas' escape failed. The rat leaped on top of him, sinking its teeth into his neck.

His screams ricocheted off the walls as Tray slammed the door shut, held his back to it. "Take the flashlight and get a chair or somethin' to keep this door shut, Wendy!"

Wendy blinked, swathed with shock and horror.

The creature pushed against the door.

"Hey! Anybody! Help us!" Tray shouted.

Footsteps pounded the floor and a few of the truckers appeared. The door to the storage flew open and Tray stumbled forward, dropped the flashlight, slammed into a metal counter, knocking the wind out of him.

Gasping for air, he heard the truckers screaming. Slow to rise, he tried calling to Wendy, but his words only whispered. Coughing, sucking in more air, he tried again: "Wendy, you near?"

No response.

A body knocked Tray back down. He heard the guy moan and a he caught a whiff of copper.

Blood.

Tray also smelled decay. The rat moved toward the front room. "Shit!" Slower than the last he somehow managed to pull himself upright. He located the flashlight, scooped it up. Its beam speared two twitching bodies with their throats ripped wide open.

His stomach soured.

A scream shot through the darkness.

He needed to find Wendy and save his own ass. Old age cursed his body, reminding him of his age, reminding him his age of being a youngster was non-returnable.

Stepping into the front room he might as well have taken a ticket from the little red dispenser, awaiting his turn as a customer in a human butcher shop.

Pieces of bodies scattered the counter, on tables, on the floor as if a tornado made of barbed wire came through. The windows glistened with splattered blood. Three truckers out of the group, still alive, one holding a chair, one holding a broom handle, while the other gripped a crowbar to fight the creature. Tray had no idea where the guy found the crowbar.

Luck, he supposed.

No sign of Wendy.

The barricade of chairs and tables behind the men was shoved out of the way as the front door opened. The men lost their balance, smacking the floor.

The children entered.

"Holy shit!" *Time to go! Could he get to his truck safely? Where the hell was Wendy? Was she dead?*

Tray heard bare feet slapping the kitchen floor.

The children must have broken through the back door. Had no one thought to barricade it? Including himself? Damn if he could remember!

"Come out come out wherever you are!" a child's voice slithered out of the kitchen.

Tray crested the side of the diner wall and slipped through the double-glass door of the adjunct convenience store while the rat and the children fed on the smorgasbord of truckers. A barricade of more chairs and tables had been shoved against its entrance/exit door.

Thank God...

Though, when he ran down an aisle, attempting to locate something to shove through the door handles, preventing the rat or the children from breaking through, the entrance/exit doors crashed open.

Three children stood in the doorway.

Gripping cleavers, grinning from ear to ear, their bodies cast a wide shadow over the old man in the truck's headlights.

"Going somewhere, old man?"

Tray rocketed to the back of the store, found a door, flung it wide.

Wendy and the convenience store cashier, Julie, were huddled together against the wall behind boxes.

"Wendy! You're alive!" Tray said.

He scanned the room for something to block the door. A chair sat to his left. Tray grabbed it, propped it against the door with the headrest snug under the doorknob.

"She's in shock." Julie wrapped her plump arms around Wendy. The cashier wasn't far from shock, either. A lock of blonde hair hung in front of her eyes.

"Is there a backdoor out of this place?"

"Yeah. You'll have to move boxes out of your way to get to the next room. You'll see the backdoor. Its locked." She reached into her pocket, fumbled for the right key on her keyring. "Here's the key."

"Thanks."

"Those kids have broken in, haven't they? I heard those men scream. It sounded horrible..."

"They're in, and we need to get the hell out!"

Julie helped Wendy up.

"My little Eddie...Wh—what's happened to him?" Wendy's looked at Tray for an explanation.

Tray had not an answer. He didn't know what to say.

Between the two, the truck driver and the clerk, they managed to drag Wendy out of the back door. But not before Tray took a peek outside first, cautious of any evil waiting.

"Listen. Stay here. I'm gonna try and get my truck." Tray told the women, and then slid along the wall and glanced the corner. No kids in sight. His truck sat idling, headlights blazing. Quickly, he slipped inside, greeted by the last bit of *House of the Rising Sun* by the Animals on the radio.

He switched the semi into gear.

He drove the rig around to the back of the truck stop, but did not see a hair of the women. They had vanished.

"The hell are they?" He slapped the steering wheel and got out of the truck. "Wendy? Julie?"

Two heads peaked around a large green dumpster. "Over here!"

"What are you all doin'?" Tray shouted.

"Hiding."" Julie said. "I was afraid you'd be gone too long and those kids would see us."

"C'mon, let's get gone!"

Julie helped Wendy into the passenger seat of the truck then climbed the back where it contained Tray's bed, his clothes and his small cooler.

"Hold onto your hairpins ladies, we're outta here." Tray shifted the rig into gear and drove around the front and onto the road.

In the side mirror, Tray saw a horde of children pour outside of the truck stop and try to take chase.

Tray mashed the accelerator.

***

History Lesson Number Two

The day before Kabul found his death in Woodbin he had a dream. He had stopped to sleep on the forest floor and gaze at the full moon. The creatures lurking at night spoke, letting him know of their existence. The shrill sounds of the crickets chirped out of the darkness. A hoot owl sat high up on a branch. Off in the distance, up on a hill, a wolf howled.

Kabul had been a drifter for many years. His grandfather had taught him how to play the pipe and he became very good. Sometimes, whenever he reached a village, he would stand and play. Most of the villagers would come and listen. They would admire his talent and wished they could play such beautiful notes as he. Kabul even had a few young ladies giving him the eye, while he would stand there. Handsome, sincere, a pleasant man with a big heart, Kabul loved to make people happy. Playing the pipe for villagers seemed to do the trick, as well as helping to block out his depression.

Two years prior he lost his wife of seven years, his two children, and his grandfather in a raging fire caused by a terrible storm. Lightning had struck a tree, setting it on fire. It fell on one villager's home, crushing it and the two people inside. The flames licked the air and spread.

Kabul's home had been next in line of the blaze. His children's room, closest to the fire, became engulfed. Kabul barely escaped death, carrying his lovely wife in his arms.

Helpless, he stood listening to his children's screams as they perished in the fire.

One by one, the houses in the village of Eastknob took fire until the whole village burned to the ground.

Tears streaming from his eyes, Kabul laid his beautiful wife on the grass. Smoke had filled her lungs. She hacked and coughed, not getting enough oxygen in her lungs to stay alive. Kabul held her close, wishing God would not take her from him.

However, Kabul thought God failed him. He cursed Him. Stood shouting at the skies, asking why He would take his only flesh and blood and wife.

No response came.

Kabul buried his wife under an oak tree, the exact place where they had met and where they would always bring their children to play. More tears streamed from his eyes.

All alone, no one to comfort him and whisper, "I love you, my dear husband." No children to hold in his arms and watch their faces brighten. This terrible accident forced him to decide to become a drifter, staying far away as possible of the pain of Eastknob.

Kabul wanted to drag the bodies of his children out of the rubble, but could not bear the fact when his hands touched their bones, they would turn to dust. One villager, a man who had children of his own and a wife of ten years, tried to sift through the disaster, only to find his youngest child's skull still intact.

As the memories of the horror came back to haunt Kabul, he fell into a nightmare. His dreams brought back the screams of his children when they were dying. In this particular setting his wife had also been trapped. Her shrieks pierced his ears. Kabul tried to run into the flames and save them, not caring whether his flesh burned or not. He could not move his legs and feet. Something pressed against his chest, a large hand, not allowing him to move.

He screamed awake, a cold sweat drenched his skin, and opened his eyes. The sun had not crested the horizon. Out of the corner of his eye, something moved within the trees. His hand gripped the handle of his knife. Knowing the use of it in defense would hardly be applicable, the blade being dull, it did allow somewhat of a comfort for danger.

He stood.

The small fire he used for heat had almost gone out. The wind blew a cold air. Spring time had almost fulfilled its destiny for the year and summer neared. He couldn't understand the temperature being so low.

Out of the dark, a voice reached his ears. A whisper of words he could barely make out.; then it came again. Recognizable.

Impossible! he thought.

It returned. He wondered if he should pursue it. Kabul seriously wondered if it could be a robber throwing his voice, acting as a ghost and trying to be haunting. In turn, Kabul should rise, run away in fear, only to witness the robber jump out of the dark and rob him. After contemplating, listening to the softness of the voice's tone, he chose not to. He decided to track the voice down. Kabul knew no robber could do this. Most would as soon cut you, take your belongings and run off, rather than play games.

Kabul walked through the woods and continued to hear the voice, drifting along the breeze, now, calling out his name. Long, drawn out, it sent a chill down to his spine. As he came upon a cave, he saw an orange glow throwing dancing shadows on the inner walls. He licked his lips.

What is this? A form of black magic or sorcery?

The voice spoke his name.

Cautiously, he stepped inside. The feeling of loss crashed down on him, for perhaps the hundredth time in his life. There by the glow of a small fire, his beautiful wife sat on a large rock. The skin on her face was smooth and beautiful as if the flames had never touched it.

She smiled. "Hello, my dear."

"How...How is it you are here? You've been gone for, for—"

"Quite some time. Yes."

"I don't understand, I...I buried you."

"Yes. And I have risen to bring you grave news you must spread. It is very important you do so. Many will die if you do not."

"What are you asking of me? I am not a savior. I could not save you or the children." He choked back a sob. "What is there left for me to accomplish besides walking these lands and playing my pipe?"

Her smile brightened and the glow highlighted it. "Kabul, my dear husband, you do not know of your true talent." She stood up. "You can save a village. It will make you feel so much better. Do it in a remembrance of your love for me." She walked over, standing a foot away from him. "Kabul, you must go to the village of Woodbin. It isn't far from here, you will know the way. Follow your heart. I will be with you, guiding you along."

Kabul wanted to hold her in his arms. "I am so sorry I could not save you or the children from death. Many times I so wanted to take my life and slice open my wrist and let the life flow out of my flesh and die so I could be at your side. But ...I am a coward."

"Oh, my poor, Kabul." Her head tipped to the side. "You are a brave man. You have always been brave. You should not think of such dread. You have a job to do. You can save the villagers of Woodbin from an infestation of rats."

"Rats?"

"They have escaped from a desolate city and are very hungry. They will attack Woodbin, cause havoc, and eat the villager's food. Perhaps attack the villagers themselves." Beth placed her hand on the side of Kabul's face. "I know you will do the right thing, won't you?"

Kabul could actually feel the warmth of his dead wife's hand. How, he had no clue. He wanted to take her into his arms and hold her forever. His arms moved to do so, but she stepped back and regained her composure sitting on the large rock.

"Please follow through with this Kabul. For me?"

"Why do you ask of this? Why not someone else? Who sent you here?"

"Who sent me, is not important. Look inside your heart and you will know who has. He is the Almighty. I ask you this because I want your life to be better as a hero. You deserve more. I know you tried to save me and our children. I love you, and I will always love you."

"And I love you."

"I must go, Kabul, I must return to the land of the dead."

"You can't stay?" His voice pleaded.

"I'm so sorry, Kabul. My time is up. I must return." Right before his eyes, her body faded away, leaving behind: "I will always love ...you."

Kabul's legs became mush. He plopped down on the floor of the cave, hung his head, and wept. As he sobbed, he did not notice the ghostly silhouette with ten horns and seven heads close by, muffling a sinister laugh.

Kabul cried himself awake.

He laid on his back and the sun's rays blinded him.

Had it all a dream?

Stretching, he rose, gathered his belongings together and saw something familiar lying by the burnt-out fire: His wife's necklace, a turquoise rock threaded through a thin chain he had made for her on the day of their wedding.

He picked it up, rolled the rock between his first finger and thumb, remembering when he made it. A tear fell from his eye.

Kabul stood, dropped the necklace in his pocket, and set out for Woodbin.

Chapter 31

Tray's semi hugged the road. Clouds of smoke spilled out of its twin pipes. BAILEY'S FINEST CHEW IN THE TERRITORY! NOW IN WINTERGREEN AND WATERMELON FLAVORS! illustrated both sides of the trailer, along with a grinning cartoon face of a guy wearing a straw hat giving a "thumbs-up".

Tray glanced at Wendy. "How you doin' over there?"

Wendy slumped in the seat and her head rested against the passenger side window. She mumbled.

"Wendy? Listen, I need ya to be strong, hon. Can you do that for me?"

"Yeah. I—I think so." Her face contracted; she started crying. "Oh, Eddie ..." Witnessing her son ripped wide open and a creature evolved from his body continued to chill her blood.

"Wendy, you have to realize Eddie isn't with us anymore. That thing back there took 'em. Whatever it was. I sure wish I knew what the frog shit is goin' on. It's like the world's collapsing."

"He was just a little boy, Tray. My baby!" Her voice cracked. "How can...How the hell can that happen?"

"Don't know. Please try and be strong. Do you have any other kids we need to find? Do you want to try and stop by your place?"

Wendy wiped the tears away with both hands. "There's my, my husband."

"Is he at home?"

"He should be. Unless he's still down at Scooter's."

"Scooter's?"

"The bar downtown. He should be home by now, I suppose."

"Well, then, let's git over to your house and see." Tray glanced over his shoulder at Julie, then back to the road. "What about you, ma'am? Need to go by your place, too?"

"No. I'm good," Julie said. "I live by myself."

"Okay. Wendy, direct me to where you need to go."

Wendy ran her fingers through her hair. "Follow this road. It's, it's a few miles away."

Tray flipped on the CB radio only to find static. "That's odd." He switched channels, waiting to hear a voice. Finally, one popped up.

The guy who spoke was frantic, startling all three riding in the truck.

"—s anyone on here? Come back? This is Ken Marsh. We've got a situation out here at the North Falls Commons. I'm droppin' off my trailer, pickin' up another. There are children running around here with knives. Hear me? They're killin' people right and left! Anyone on here? Any—"

Tray grabbed the microphone. "Hey, this is Tray. Stay inside your truck, Ken. Don't git out. Understand?"

"Tray? God it's good to hear a voice on here! Been trying for a half an hour to find someone. It's a blood bath here! I dropped off my trailer and heard a scream come outta the warehouse. Knew it was strange not seeing a guard at the gate. Hell, I thought the guy mighta went to dinner."

"Listen to me. Can you get your rig started?" Tray asked.

Ken didn't respond.

"Kenny? You there?"

A few seconds slipped by before: "Yeah. I'm here," Ken replied. "Sorry. Thought I heard something right outside my door. I peeked out and saw nothing. I don't think those kids have seen me, man. When I had heard that scream I ran over to the warehouse doors and looked inside. Wished I hadn't. Terrible scene. Horrible! A gang of those youngin's were taking turns one stabbing some poor guy in the face. And there was something else in that warehouse, Tray. I wouldn't believe it if I hadn't seen it with my own two eyes…" his voice trailed off.

"Kenny? What was it?" What'd you see?" Tray glanced at Wendy. She held her hands over her ears.

"God in Heaven…There were two huge rats gnawing on a pile of corpses. They were feeding on them. God-awful amount of blood…enough to fill a pond."

A flash of the rat attacking Thomas. Tray's stomach soured. "Look. Git yourself outta there. Ya hear? You need to get your rig moving'. I'm packing two passengers and rollin' down I-30, headed to a young lady's house in the 'burbs. Gotta see if her husband is there. Why don't you meet me in the parking lot at the new shopping center in Hampshire. Shouldn't be far from you."

"Oh God…I see them out there, looking for me." Ken said. "One is holding a huge knife…The other one is holding a crowbar. Man, their frickin' eyes! They're leaking and are as black as coal!"

Wendy placed her hands over her ears. She did not want to hear this. No more horror. She didn't know if her nerves could take much more. First she watched Gerald's death. Then trying to barricade the doors to stop the gang of children. Finally, witness to Eddie's death and transformation into a giant rat.

"Kenny," Tray said. "Get out of there! Run those creatures over with your truck!"

"Tray, they found me. They're right in front of my truck."

"Start that rig up and run 'em over, Ken. Right the now!"

"Oh crap…Oh crap…This thing ain't startin'! Something's

wrong!" Glass shattered. "Good God! They're climbing into my truck! Help me, Tray! Help me …*somebody!* Stay the hell away from me! STAY THE HELL AW—"

"Ken! *Kenny!*" Tray spat.

Julie held onto herself and shuddered.

Silence filled the cab.

"I—I tried to help this guy." Tray let the microphone drop. "I—I tried like hell to." He sighed, rubbed a hand across his face.

A voice shrilled on the radio. "Come out come out wherever you are?" A giggle. "Where are ya, Tray? Mr. Kenny don't wanna play no more. He," — giggles — "pooh-poohed and pee-peed his pants. Not a very nice thing to do. Needs to be potty trained." Laughter. "Tray? We want to play a game. All of us here. Let's see if we can play hide and go seek. You all hide and we will seek. The winner gets to collect the player's head. You in, Tray? Tray? What's wrong, cat got your tongue? You know, if a rat gets your tongue it'll rip it out of your mouth and eat it. Did you know that, Tray?"

Tray continued to be quite.

"If we ever find you we'll also play 'pin Mr. Ken's entrails on Tray and Wendy and Julie's bee-hind. You should feel how squishy and wet they are …" A shriek of laughter crackled through the speakers. "Benny said they taste *ohsogoodohsogood!* Reminded him of when he used to eat spaghetti—minus the parmesan cheese. Didn't much favor it. Gave him the Hershey Squirts! It also gave him—"

Tray switched the channel, sick of listening to those kids. He glanced at his passenger Wendy, her hands plastered over her ears, her eyes shut, wracked with sobs. Julie wrapped her arms around herself, rocking back and forth.

Silence inside the cab during their travel until they spotted two vehicles off to the shoulder. A small Honda and an SUV. Three children stood over an old woman sprawled out on the pavement.

Chapter 32

During the time when Kenny's frantic voice blurted through the air waves into Tray's truck, Martha sat in the SUV and watched for Dean and Shro to emerge from the woods.

All this horror crashed into her and for the first time tonight, her emotions broke loose and she sobbed. Memories of Penny returned. The girl would always come down and play with her dolls. Martha loved children. Penny's parents, on several occasions, had invited her out to dinner. Most of the time, she accepted. Those were really good times. Really great times.

Martha popped open the glove compartment, searching for a tissue. None there, but a few napkins. She blew her nose, closing her eyes, shutting out the world.

What the hell happened? What changed the events of time? How can something, whatever it is, happen? Were we really in the book of Revelations? Children killing adults? Absurd! It was hard to swallow these facts!

She opened her eyes.

The small face of one of those evil kids pressed his face on the window. He ran his tongue across the glass and grinned.

"Hi, Martha."

She gasped.

"Can," he chewed off the tip of his first finger, spit it out, and ran it over the glass, smearing a line of blood, "Martha come out and play?"

From the other side, through the driver's side window, another kid appeared. The girl kissed the window, leaving a bloody print.

Flailing her arms and legs she danced a jig and sung, "Ding dong, the witch is dead! Ding dong, the witch is dead! *Ding* dong!" She waved. "Hello, Martha!"

Martha heard a sound and turned to see the point of a large knife tapping on the window.

"Get away from me!" she cursed, drew back, the gear shift stuck into her spine.

"Get away?" the boy asked. "I thought you wanted to play with us. You played with Penny, why not play with us?" He stuck out his bottom lip. "We play fair."

Martha drew back and the gear shift pressed into her back.

"Martha, come out, come out," the boy sung.

"Not by the hair of my old chinny-chin-chin," the girl mimicked Martha's voice.

"Or I'll huff and I'll puff," the boy sung. "And cave your head in!" He moved out of the way and a bat crashed into the windshield.

Martha shrieked, held her hands over her eyes, squeezed them shut.

"Come on out Martha! We want to see how much blood is left in a decrepit old woman's body!"

Martha dropped her guard just in time to see the one wielding the bat, another boy, half the flesh on his face flapping with his every move, charge the SUV. Again, she squeezed her eyes shut and covered her face as the bat hit the glass a second time.

A third attack left pieces in Martha's lap.

The side passenger window burst. The sting of glass sliced into her hands. By her hair she was yanked across the driver's seat and onto the pavement.

She opened her eyes.

"Martha, we're going to play with you *longer* than Penny did." The boy who spoke to her through the window said, the girl and one holding the bat stood beside him. "How about we show you a better game called Operation? Ever heard of it? It's where you try and pull out, say, the Adam's apple, your stomach, the bread basket, and—"

"A beating heart," the little girl said, pulling out an ice pick from her pocket.

"A wishbone," the one with the bat added.

"—and the butterflies in your stomach," the knife-handler finished.

"But first," the boy with the bat smiled, "we need to see what's in that cranium of yours. How much history do you really know, Martha, in all of your seventy years here on Earth?"

Headlights illuminated the kid as he raised the bat over his head.

Chapter 33

"Holy shit!" Tray said, pressing on the brake pedal.

Wendy raised her head. Her eyes were wide.

In the headlight beam an old woman was being attacked.

Julie moved forward. "We need to help that woman!"

"Way ahead of you." Tray laid on the horn. The blare made the children stop their attack and gaze at the truck.

Tray said, "Look back there and see if you see a tackle box."

Julie scavenged through the back, located it and handed it to Tray. "Thank you." Tray flipped open the metal latches and reached inside. "I never thought I'd have to use this. Guess it's as good a time as any. My paw gave me this when I was younger. Taught me how to shoot. I have his shotgun, but it's no help. Damn thing is in my closet back home." He gazed at Wendy. "I remember your cook not having much luck with his gun. But I'm not going out there empty-handed. You two wait here. Julie, take care of Wendy. I'm gonna try and save that woman and keep moving."

Julie nodded.

Tray stepped outside, shut the truck's door.

Wendy watched Tray move toward the kids and the old woman sprawled in the street. She thought about Shro. She needed to find him. She prayed he was still alive.

"Get away from the woman, hear me?" Tray pointed the pistol. The kids did not move.

"I said get away from her right *now* or each of your heads will be target practice!" Tray could only wish his words were effective. His hand holding the pistol shook from fear of these kids.

The kids smiled, backed away.

"You okay, ma'am?"

"I-I'm fine," she replied, out of breath.

The three children began giggling.

"What's so damn funny?" Tray spat.

The kid holding the large knife said, "You. You're funny."

"What?"

"You're funny! You want to be a cowboy?"

"Or a police man?" the girl said.

"Or an army man?" the kid holding a baseball bat said.

"Look here: I'm gonna take this woman," he helped her up, taking her hand, "and we are gonna leave. Got it?"

The three kids suddenly became silent. Their giggling ceased and their bottom lips stuck out.

"But we only want to play, Tray."

His brows furrowed. "How do you know my name?"

"We."

"Just."

"Do."

The one holding the bat started tapping his palm with its broken end. Flesh flaked onto the ground.

"We only want to play." The children repeated in unison, then stepped forward.

***

Dean folded his legs, sobbed, wrapped his arms around himself.

Memories of his beloved played over and over through his brain: The day they first met, listening to the jazz band at the coffee shop; the day they were married; the day they took the cruise to the islands; the times they would be so passionate in their love-making; and the day they decided to have a child. Now their life together was a collection of keepsakes tucked away in a box and placed up in the attic.

Why would somebody do this to her? Angry, he wished to kill the person responsible for his beloved's death.

"Hey, man …you, uh, gonna be okay?" Shro inquired, not really know the words to say to Dean. The guy just lost his wife and found her impaled in a field. *Who the hell would do this?* Shro thought of Wendy and prayed she was safe. He needed to get to her as soon as possible.

Dean didn't answer. Shro repeated the question.

Wracked with sadness, Dean stayed huddled down, unmoving.

"Dean …Man, we're gonna have to call the cops or somethin'"

Dean wiped his face, stood. He reached down and picked up the shotgun.

"Dean. We, uh, may need to get to police. This is terrible."

"Do ya think?" Dean's head whipped around. "Somebody is gonna pay for this, Shro!" he said through gritted teeth. "Why me? Why the hell did somebody do this to me, huh? Why did they take Rachael from me? Huh?"

"I, I don't know, ma—"

"Somebody took my wife away from me and damned if they aren't gonna pay!" His voice echoed.

Shro saw something shift in the darkness, take shape, and swung his flashlight, bringing back a sight he did not want. "Uh-oh. Dean. We ain't alone."

Dean followed Shro's beam, saw it, and his finger rested on the trigger of the shotgun.

Five dark-headed children stepped out between the trees. Black blood oozed from ripped wounds on their face. They pulled back their lips, revealing their choppers.

"Hello, Dean," one said.

"Hello, Shro," another said.

"Did you see what we got to do today? We couldn't wait to show you guys!"

Dean only glared at them. These were the kids who murdered his wife.

"Wanna play a game? We want to play." The group of kids circled around Rachael's impaled corpse.

One stepped forward, gave an uptick of his chin. "Rachael was a lot of fun to play with."

Chuckling came from the kids.

Dean gritted his teeth.

"You shoulda seen how we did this to your beloved. It was classic move! See," the kid used his hands and arms to explain, "Gary lay on the side of the road and played dead. Right, Gary?"

"Yup,' a short kid admitted.

"We all had to play paper, rock, scissors to see who would have to do it, and Gary lost. Poor guy. Can't win for losin'. Did you know his momma tried to drown him in the tub tonight?"

Gary giggled.

"Oh, but you showed her, didn't you, Gary?"

"Yeah. She told me I needed to take a bath before I went to bed," Gary replied. "I said okee-dohkee, Mommy. She ran the bath water, dumped some bubble bath in it and let me bathe myself. But, hee—hee, she tried to sneak up, ease into the bathroom when she thought I wasn't lookin' and force my head under the water." Gary threw his head back and belly-laughed. "Boy, you should have seen the look on her face when I stuck my daddy's straight razor in her left eye. Never knew the eyeball would pop out so easily. Pretty rad!"

"Pop!" one of the other kids echoed.

Another kid hooked his finger and stuck it in his mouth, quickly yanking it out, making a "popping" sound.

The children laughed.

"It was so damn funny, Dean and Shro!" Gary continued. "Mommy bled so much the bathwater turned a bright red color. Never saw red bubble bath before."

Shro gasped.

Dean held the shotgun, his finger on the trigger.

"I cut her up in so many pieces, Dean. Yessiree I did. You could say the meat fell off the bone!"

The children cackled.

"Which one of you did this?" Dean demanded, pointing at his dead wife. "Huh? Which one of you monsters did this?"

"Well, if you had let me finished the story," the boy who had begun narrating Rachael's death before Gary chimed in about killing his mom, said, "I was going to give you a step-by-step log of how Rachael died. However, by the look on your face you probably don't want to know, right?" If not for his missing eyebrow torn away above his left eye, he could have raised both eyebrows, instead of the single. "The truth is, Dean, we *all* took part in her demise. If it helps, she only screamed four times."

Each child held up four fingers. One had a bit of trouble, since the girl missed a couple of digits.

"We tried to make her scream more, but I think she held back."

"She was one tough cookie, your wife!" Gary said, slapping his knee, giggling.

"Now," the narrator said, "we all want to know this, Dean and Shro: Will you be able to outdo Rachael's screams? Will both of you fellas be able to let lose a guttural scream, one that starts in the stomach and claws its way out of the throat? We already have a bet going on to see which one of us can torture you men the best. Winner takes both of your heads. We might even get a pat on the back from our master."

Each child brandished long knives from behind their backs.

Dean raised the shotgun. When the first child rocketed forward, the girl lost her face.

***

The second Tray lifted the pistol to shoot the kid, pain exploded in his arm. His pistol bounced off the ground. Another swing of the bat took Tray to the ground. He thought for sure he could help the lady back to the truck safely without a fight. *Thought* he could have.

The lady stumbled back when the kid hit Tray. She picked up the pistol. "Get back!"

The one with the bat retreated with a smile. "There's more to come, Martha. Why make it hard on yourself? Play with us! We have so many other games to play besides *Operation*."

"Get the hell back, child!" Martha spat.

"Tsk-tsk-tsk," The kid holding the long blade said. "Testy, are we?"

"Tray? Can you stand?" She kept the pistol aimed at the kids and helped Tray up.

"Dammit, it hurts!" Tray rubbed his arm.

"Did he break any bones?"

"Don't think so."

"Leave us alone!" Martha told the kids.

The three kids laughed and mocked. "Weeve us awone! Weeve us awone!

"Let's see how much you bleed." the boy with the long blade stepped forward. "We already know your old bones will break under the thin flesh you wear if bat-boy here hits you harder. Both of you are too old. You need to be put out of your misery. The world is shifting to bright new world. And you two aren't invited to the opening."

A thunderclap, the blast of a shotgun, echoed in the distance.

"Huh. Someone else is having a bit of a party, too," the boy said.

***

Wendy and Julie had sat in the truck watching the boy attack Tray, knocking him down.

"We need to do something, Julie." Wendy hadn't spoke for some time, still reveling in the horror back at the truck stop. Feeling the horrid feeling of Eddie turned into one of those creatures. Reality smacked her. "Is there anything else back there we can use for a weapon?"

"Hang on a sec." Julie said. "Got a steel bar back here."

"Good. See another one?"

"No … Wait. I found something else." She gave Wendy a crowbar. "You, um, going to be okay?'

Wendy forced a grin. "Y-Yeah. Think so. We need to help Tray. Can't just sit here."

They slipped out of the truck, saw Martha helping Tray up, aiming the pistol at the kids, and heard the sound of the shotgun.

***

The blast from the shotgun shaved the girl's face off, knocked the child to the ground. Oozing eye sockets glared at Dean. "Owee, mister!"

Dean reloaded the shotgun.

She started to bawl, manifesting into a cackle, followed by a loud guffaw, a reverberation in the clearing. She got up.

"You hurt Mindy, Dean!" Gary shouted. "You ain't playin' fair!"

"Damn right I'm not. Don't come any closer or another one of you will lose your head!"

"Look, kids," the narrator waved a hand, "a gunslinger, our Dean."

The children burst out laughing. One of them took a chance and rushed Dean.

The shotgun blast burrowed a hole in the kid's face, knocking the body end over end, smacking the ground. The head lopped off as the body rose back up.

Two of the kids swerved around Rachael's corpse and slammed into Shro's blindside, shoving him down. Two more kids rushed Dean before he could reload and stabbed him in the back.

***

"Get away from those two," Wendy snapped, wielding the crowbar. Tray and Martha twisted their heads backward.

"Wendy! No! Get back to my truck!" Tray warned.

"I'm not lettin' these kids kill you two," Wendy said.

Julie helped Martha pull Tray up.

"Well, well, more meat to put on the grill!" The child with the blade said.

Bat-boy stood there, gripping the handle of the bat, tapping the end of it on his palm. "How tough are your bones, Wendy?"

"I said stay back!"

"Your poor Gerald couldn't comprehend what is going on in his itty-bitty pebble he called a brain. Things are changing, Wendy. The world is shifting forward, a bright new world is on the horizon."

"What are you talking about? She thought of Eddie and what he explained before changing into the rat. Terror filled her insides at the pictures she recollected.

"It is the beginning to an end, Wendy," the girl added. "You cannot stop it. You cannot control it. It is Earth's destiny."

"Destiny?"

"Yep. You've been given a ticket to come aboard the apocalyptic train and be delivered to your deaths."

***

The children were winning.

Two more emerged from the group and tackled Dean. Pain sliced through Dean's body. He watched the wooden point of the stake tear a hole in his chest, splattering his face with his own blood. Screaming, he let go of the gun, fell to his knees for the second time tonight.

Shro fought to rise, two small kids forcing him down. He smelled their decay. They laughed while a warmth spilled across his face.

"Stay down, Shroster. You'll be a-okay in a few. Lie there and watch Dean become a king," a voice whispered into his ear. "Ain't nuffin' you can do, Shro, but wait your turn." Giggle.

"Get off ...*me!* Dean! Fight them off!" Shro shouted, not aware of what they had done to Dean until one of the kids moved to the side, revealing the wooden stack shoved through the man's body.

Shro gasped.

Dean gasped for air, tasting copper as blood filled his throat and mouth.

"You're gonna be a king, Dean!" a voice cracked across the field, unknown which child spoke. "You and Rachael, king and queen, *forever!*"

Dean gasped, barely sucking in a mouth full of air to fill the single lung which had not been punctured from the sharp end of the wooden pole. His vision blurred. His body grew numb. The world dimmed, but not before he witnessed four robed figures gazing at him, hovering in the sky, each tucked inside a transparent sphere.

***

"Who or what told you to cause this horror, murdering innocent people?"

"Well," the child holding the blade grinned, "it wasn't up to us. We are simply doing what we are told. It is the one who will lead us to the damnation of Earth. It is the musician."

"The *who?*" Julie asked.

"The one," the girl said, "who leads us. Our master. The musician."

"Oh, look, here he comes," Bat-boy said.

Wendy saw the trees quiver as something black slipped out of them. She had to blink twice because her brain tried to make out a splotch of darkness moving on its own. The thing twisted, turned and shot upward.

The air changed, becoming colder. Goose bumps plagued the flesh of Wendy, Tray, Martha and Julie. The hair on the back of their necks rose.

Objects and living beings on Earth give off shadows, this particular one did not. Circling like a vulture over their heads, it bore no mercy for the pain the children had caused the humans. It would not be reasoned with, pleaded with, from anyone to stay alive in the shift forward to an apocalypse. It had witnessed the king impaled next to the queen of the apocalypse and was quite happy.

The shadow landed, first shaping into an oblong creature. Dozens of eyes surfaced, blinked. A quick morph and a hooded silhouette stood on the road.

A skeletal face grinned.

"Good Lord." Martha said under her breath.

Wendy and Julie were speechless.

Tray's mouth hung open.

The head of the silhouette split, blossoming seven screaming heads, each attached to their own branch. Horns grew from their craniums and multiple claws flanked its sides.

Tray said. "Everyone. Get back to the truck!"

The three children smiled.

***

Somehow Shro managed to throw both figures off of him, scramble across the grass on all fours and pick up the shotgun. But not before he had listened to Dean's screams until he thought his ears would bleed. Shro watched as they slit Dean open, unloading his intestines onto the ground. He knew he could not help the guy. No way to save him.

The ones who had impaled Dean stood him upright beside his beloved. Two lovers who were not laid side by side in the earth, but posed as monuments of horror. Their mouths agape, their eyes rolled to show their whites; their facial expressions, frozen with pain.

Shro witnessed more terror.

Two of the children who had caught Dean's shotgun blast decided to shed their skin. Shro watched them both tear free of their flesh, revealing large rats. For an added feature they fed on the entrails of both impaled humans.

Shro's ears and stomach could not take it any longer.

He plunged into the darkness of the woods, praying he would not stumble and crash into a tree. Laughter chased him as he ran toward light spilled between the trees.

Chapter 34

Emerging, Shro saw an older guy shoving three women toward a semi-truck. One of them, Martha, One, his wife. He also recognized Julie who worked at the Truck Stop.

"Wendy!" Shro shouted.

Wendy whipped around.

Shro grinned.

"Shro!"

Shro started toward her, stopped, taking notice to a horrid-looking creature, two boys and one girl, each one of those demonic kids. Each one noticed him.

"What the hell is th—?"

"C'mon! Get in the truck!" The older guy waved him over.

Shro took a few steps and watched the girl laugh as she rocketed forward, a long metal yarn needle in her grip.

The old guy lifted a pistol and shot her through the eye. She wavered, not smacking the pavement, and took a leap, crashing down on Julie.

She screamed as the girl jammed the long needle into her back over and over.

The old guy stuck the barrel of the gun against the girl's head and shot her point-blank, knocking her off Julie.

The girl took a roll across the pavement, rose back up, growled.

The guy took another aim and the girl's head exploded, raining brain matter and blood. Her body dropped like a sack of severed heads.

Wendy and Tray helped Julie off the ground. Her face ashen, the back of her neck was caked with blood and a red spray moistened the pavement.

"Julie!" Wendy said. "Julie! Are you okay?"

Julie did not respond.

"I think she's dead, Wendy," Tray said. "That girl must have hit Julie's jugular."

"No…she can't be."

"Wendy….she's gone. Let's shit-and-get." Tray saw Martha climbing into the truck, noticed Shro.

"The hell are you waiting for? Get in the truck!" The old guy once again waved Shro over.

Shro hadn't realized he had stood there and watched that girl attack Julie. Now he took off. Halfway to his destination pain exploded on the side of his face and he crashed the ground. Laughter from his assailant was abruptly cut-off when a shot echoed. Shro rolled over, saw a blurry vision of a baseball bat lying next to him.

One of the boys lay sprawled ten feet away in the grass.

The kid must have launched the bat through the air…

The boy started rising.

***

When Tray dropped the kid who attacked Shro the other boy charged him.

Tray pulled the trigger, separating the kid's fingers from his hand. The blade the kid had held pin—wheeled through the air, dropped, bounced off the pavement.

The boy glared.

Tray pulled the trigger again and the kid's face blew off. Bits and pieces of skin and cartilage sprayed the ground. Strands of flesh hung when he turned to look at Tray.

A crooked smile grew under a missing nose.

The kid reached up with both hands and grabbed a fold of dangling skin on his face and ripped it away, spilling a glob of black blood. Beneath, a rat head pushed through, reminding Tray of the horror back at the truck stop. Claws pushed through the boy's fingertips and it soon tore free from its entire cocoon of flesh. A large puddle of black blood and pieces of skin lay at its feet.

Tray tried to fire the pistol again and nothing happened. "Shit!" Out of bullets. He pulled the trigger over and over — *click-click-click* — hoping to have one single bullet lodged inside the chamber to be fired.

"Out of bullets old man?" the rat creature snarled. "Surrender your flesh and blood, old man. There is nowhere to go to now, only, into your grave."

The creature advanced with claws out.

***

Shro gripped the barrel and, still lying on the ground, whipped the butt end around to smack the boy in the face, hearing a crack, knocking him to the side. He stood, balanced himself, held the weapon low by his waist, planted his feet and pulled the trigger.

Nothing happened.

Bat-boy rose up and cackled, his pointy teeth showing through a hole in his cheek, and said, "Outta bullets, fella?"

And charged.

Shro reared back and brought the butt of the gun around and smashed the kid's face, feeling the skull crack, spinning him around, knocking him to the ground. Standing over the kid, Shro smashed the butt into the boy's face until it soaked of dripping, black blood mixed with skin and hair.

***

The rat creature grabbed Tray around the throat and penned him against the side of the truck. He gasped for air. The creature smiled at Wendy through the window, licked his lips. "I wonder how you'll taste, pretty one?"

Tray gasped for air, and dropped the pistol.

"Your flesh smells delicious, old man," the rat growled. "Look at it this way, you're death will be quick …and chewy."

***

As the entity stood there still in the form of a monstrosity, watching his children murder these humans, pleasure was all his. No need to interfere, the children held their own, even if there were casualties. Each child had been reborn. Each a sinister array of revenge.

The entity grinned.

Let the savagery come from beneath their young flesh. Let them eliminate the adult population, one at a time. Piece by piece.

Gazing in the night sky, he saw The Reckoning observing his work.

Each approved with a nod.

***

Wendy had enough. These creatures had taken her only child. Damn them to hell. All of them. Opening the passenger side door, her foot touched the chrome step and, head level to the rat, she swung the crowbar as hard as she could, smashing it into the rat's skull.

The creature squealed dropped Tray, held a claw over its bleeding head.

Wendy stepped onto the pavement, took another swing, sending the rat into a spin, causing it to lose its balance and fall.

Wendy bent down and helped Tray stand. He gasped for air and coughed.

"Tray? You okay?"

"Th—thanks, Wendy." Tray's voice was hoarse. "I'm ….I'm fine."

Martha stuck her head out the truck. "Behind you two!"

The girl who had lost her head, who had stabbed Julie with her sewing needle, dragged itself a few feet forward, smearing a waste of blood, sinew and fragments of bone. Then stood on all fours, a chunk of bleeding meat. Exposing the pit where her head used to be, razor-sharp teeth rotated counter-clockwise. A forked tongue diseased with blinking eyes hung form the opening. A single strand of sinew along the spine grew, an overgrown pincher at its end snapped at the air.

"Hey! Let's get the hell outta here!" Shro appeared, yanking Wendy and Tray out of their shock, the metamorphism of the girl. "I don't think I killed that boy or whatever it is back there. Something was stirring inside his caved in head."

"Get in the truck!" Tray shouted.

"Are we just gonna leave Julie's body here?" Wendy asked.

"We haven't a choice. We need to get outta here."

They all slipped inside the truck. Tray put it in gear and floored the accelerator.

"Where's Dean?" Martha said.

Shro sat in the back with her, slowly shaking his head back and forth. "He's gone. They...they impaled him," he whispered.

"What did you say?" Martha blinked.

"They *impaled* him," he said even louder: "Ain't seen nothin' like it, man. They did the same to his woman."

"Rachael?" Wendy asked.

"Yeah ..."

Horrid pictures flashed in Martha's mind of the couple's impalement. Quickly, she blocked out the vision. She couldn't begin to swallow it.

"What did they do? Say again?" Tray asked.

"They impaled Dean," Shro said. "They impaled his wife. They ran a wooden pole into them and stuck the poles into the ground, posing them like a scarecrow."

Tray whipped his head around to look at Shro. Shock masked it.

Martha closed her eyes. *That dark creature looked as if plucked out of the Book of Revelations. Lucifer himself!*

Wendy's eyes widened. "Look! More children coming out of the woods!"

Kids swarmed like insects, some already shed of their cocoons of flesh, exposing their true evil form of huge rats underneath. Some were in the middle of their metamorphosis, their flesh peeling, leaving a skin-trail in their wake.

"Hold on to yer britches!" Tray pressed the accelerator and turned the wheel. "Nothin' is gonna stand in our way!"

One of the children leapt and found the step outside the passenger window and plowed his hand and arm through it, sending shards of glass inside and grabbed Wendy around the throat. The child's body dangled out of the window, trying to find the step to regain a balance with.

Another one ran in front of the truck and around to the driver's side and opened the door's handle, allowing the door to swing wide. Tray tried to catch it; failed. The kid crawled inside and started punching Tray in the face.

The truck ran onto the shoulder of the road, rolled into grass.

Shro flew out of the back and punched the kid hard. So hard, he fell out on the ground and the back wheels of the trailer crushed his small body.

He did not rise.

Shro then wrenched free the hand gripping his wife's throat, pulling three of the fingers back, hearing the digits pop out of their joints. A face of the attacker shrieked and let go. The small body fell and rolled across the pavement.

Tray grabbed the steering wheel, mashed on the accelerated, rolled back onto the road.

The entity stood in the way.

"Go to hell!" Tray shouted, switching gears.

The dark entity grinned and became transparent, its grinning skeletal face mashed into Tray's, causing his blood to chill, making him wince.

The creature disappeared.

Tray blinked. "Everyone okay?"

"No," Shro said. "I think me and Martha's okay back here."

"Wendy? You okay?" Shro placed a hand on her shoulder.

"Y—Yeah, Shro. I'm fine." She faced him, swallowed, looked into his eyes, and said: "Eddie."

"I know. I know what happened to him. Look at this."

"He hurt your ear?"

"Dean had to pry him off me." Shro quickly explained to Wendy what happened earlier. "He's savage!"

"You don't know the half of it. He's much worse now. He's one of those rats we saw, now. I saw him change into one."

Shro shook his head.

"When we were back at the diner we were attacked by a gang of kids—."

"Started that way," Tray added. "Ended up real nasty."

"—And Gerald decided to be macho or whatever and run out the door holding a pistol."

"Gerald? With a pistol? Why would he have one there at the

diner?"

"Hell if I know, Shro … Doesn't matter 'cause he's dead."

"Dead?"

"The kids killed him in cold blood. We all watched them butcher him and could do nothing."

"We barricaded the doors but they broke in," Tray explained. "Before we were able to, two of those kids got in and killed a few people."

"Including Robert and Gary."

"The young guys who were going to that uppity college?" Shro asked.

"Yeah."

"Uppity college?"

"Shro calls it one because he thinks its preppy, nose-stuck-in-the air kinda school," Wendy explained. "Better than everyone else."

"Ain't never heard a place called it before," Tray said. "Good educations have been given there. My boy went there long ago. Became an engineer."

"See?" Wendy said, directing it at Shro. "It's a good place to go."

"Well, probably not anymore," Shro replied. "I'm thinkin' all the kids in this whole town have flipped out."

"Could be," Tray added.

"Where are we goin?" Martha asked.

"I don't know. Think we'll take a trip through town."

"Me and Dean were headed to the police station, when we saw Rachael's car off to the side. It's what made us stop."

"Good thing you had. We may not have been together, you know."

Shro smiled.

Wendy returned it. "Maybe we should go to the cops. What do you all think?" Wendy asked.

"Worth a try," Tray said and shifted gears, allowing the truck to roll toward downtown Hampshire.

Chapter 35

Vacant eyes, hollow and leaking black ooze, glared at Scooter's place. A small hand gripped the umbilical cord attached to the premature baby in tow, torn from its mother's stomach. The small corpse dragged across the ground, covered in dirt and grime and filth. Never joining with any of the other kids because he never saw a one, which, evidently made him sort of a drifter, Matthew had travelled all the way from his house in Woodbury walking over large fields, passing houses, tombs of the dead with muted screams, and along the road leading into downtown Hampshire.

Step by step.

The musician had reached out to him, showing him the path of travel. The one who possessed him and rebirthing him in a pre-apocalyptic world soon to erase the human existence, a shift forward to a new form of life on the planet.

Step by step.

Matthew had an odd gift. Ghosts spoke to him, appearing out of the darkness every so often on his journey, some even persistent, pleading for help. Some were the recent dead wandering aimlessly in the street, awaiting trial from God. Some were the ones who had died on the road by a car crash, reliving the scene over and over, screaming for mercy, trapped in a form of limbo. Others were ones who had died long ago, back when the lands were primitive villages. And some were merely ghosts who haunted the Hampshire graveyard, wondering endlessly amongst the graves. Unsettled spirits who roamed and drifted through the yard, only at night.

But what could he do? He was not the musician, given the power to shove the human race into extinction. So, he ignored them, paid them no attention. His instructions consisted of murder and bloodshed, words were spoken from the musician's lips, telling him to do these horrible acts, such as when the voice of the musician drifted through the walls of his house, earlier tonight.

Matthew had been getting ready to go to bed. He kneeled down by the bedside and saying his Hail Mary's and his Our Father's all the way through.

Sometimes he would forget the entire prayer and have to start over. Not tonight. He said them without having a "brain fart", a word his mom sometimes said.

Mom had been getting ready for bed in the next bedroom. He knew if he needed help with his prayers, he could ask mom, but he really hated to bug her. God would tell him. God would help him through it. He prayed for his mom and dad. He prayed for more chocolate bars. He prayed for the ducky's at the park to still be there when he and his mom got there tomorrow so he could feed pieces of bread to them.

If you didn't watch it, they'd bite your fingers. So, under mom's supervision, Matthew had no problem at all, being very cautious.

Matthew heard his mother's last words, asking if he had brushed his teeth and said his prayers before bed before the feeling of ice coursed through his blood and a voice speaking inside of his skull, telling him there is no God, only evil to rule the land. Matthew screwed his face up in disgust, knowing those words couldn't be true. No way.

Suddenly visions of fire and torture filled his brain, shocking little Matthew, scraping his nerves raw. One picture showed a fire illuminating a screaming man being dismembered, pulled apart by four dark creatures as they slowly cut away the flesh to get to the bone. Another showed a naked lady threaded with razor wire through her flesh, attached to other tortured souls, the collage appearing a similarity of paper cut into disturbing patterns.

The entity seeped into Matthew twisting his insides, morphing him into something less human; more creature. Intense pain, Matthew opened his mouth, trying to scream, but could only whisper. Ripples formed across the skin on his back. Veins surfaced, spider-webbed his face. He could not move, his senses numb, his bones restructured themselves, breaking apart, fusing together, a reformation of evil, staving off human. The skin on his body started to decay. The ash-gray color set in as if a demented painter threw splotches on a stretched canvas.

Step by step.

After the transformation Matthew stood up and walked into his mother's room and found her long metal scissors on the dresser. Thoughts of murder raked across his brain, his instructions sent by the musician.

His mom walked out of the bathroom, wrapped only in a white towel to find her son standing there, transformed into something she could not comprehend. Something only nightmares brought. She tried to shout for her boy to stay back, but found the pain of the scissors' points cleaving into her stomach, ripping her open, while a wet red spot filled the bath towel.

Her body stumbled, fell across the bed.

Her small attacker straddled her, slicing away her skin. Before the pain ceased, before she gasped for air through a ripped open throat, she watched Matthew pulled free her unborn son from her womb. And then darkness took hold, the drapes shut covering her vision, while the show ended forever.

Matthew found the large butcher knife in the drawer in the

kitchen — one of the drawers he could now reach, since he was tall enough. He wanted to make sure he was ready before daddy got home.

Now he stood in front of Scooter's gazing up at the square sign with the title written in red over a white background, brightly lit up.

He stepped forward, swung open the front door with the stale smell of liquor and the stench of an ashtray hitting him in the face.

Chapter 36

Patty wondered where the stinking hell Scooter was. He drove Shro home, but it shouldn't have taken this long. Scooter should have been back by now.

Shro.

The guy gave her the creeps. She knew Shro loved to stare at her, as if she was a piece of meat. Maybe she needed to let his wife know he had a roaming eye, get his ass in trouble. Why the hell Wendy ended up with Shro, she'd never know.

She knew the girl could have done better.

Patty loved Scooter. He took good care of her, making sure they had a roof over their head and food on the table. She hooked up with him five years ago when he first bought the bar. It used to be called Slick's and the name said it all. Should have been called Oil and Grease because of the nasty clientele it had. Lot of guys frequented the place back then who believed in fighting to have a good time, instead of kicking back a few beers with friends, before hitting the road for home.

Scooter changed it when he took it over. He rid the place of riff-raff, the slime buckets, making the place decent for town folk. A few of the regulars from the Slick's days came back and reformed themselves you could say, not picking fights anymore. So the days brightened, money flowed.

Not great, but good.

Patty dumped the last of the empty beer bottles in the trash behind the bar and looked in the mirror. She needed to add more makeup. She knew she probably used too much, but didn't care. Scooter never minded it. Never complained, either. He referred to her as the apple of his eye.

Patty loved those words.

She poured some water in the sink, added dish soap, and started washing shot glasses. There were a lot of them tonight. Earlier, there were a few young guys who were barely twenty—five throwing down a bottle of tequila and six beers. They all left at the same time, giving more than enough pay for the booze, and a generous tip. Overall, the night was a good one, making as much as they usually did in enough for three days. Patty figured Scooter would be very pleased when he saw the numbers. God knew they needed to get their other car up and running. It had been down for over a month with transmission trouble and to get it fixed cost more than either of them had thought. If Scooter had the tools, and if they had a garage, he could have done the work himself. Scooter used to be a mechanic and pretty darn good one.

Patty spied the bowling trophies lined up over the mirror and smiled. Scooter had won each one. A good husband with great talent. She was proud of her Scooter.

Patty bent down to carefully pick a piece of glass off the floor when she heard the front door open. Hadn't she locked it? Damn. She'd have to turn away a customer.

She stood up and began to mouth the words, "We're closed", then froze. A small figure stood there holding onto —what the hell? A cold fear swirled inside her gut — dead baby. Covered in dried blood, the small figure lifted his lips, revealing pointed teeth.

The smell of decay whisked inside the bar.

Chapter 37

If Barry could reverse history this minute — or this second — he probably would have. However, as a product of what he had been throughout the years, the way he continues to be, stemmed from life with his mother. His addiction to playing with children in a leisurely, obscene fashion, and killing them, could never be undone. Turning back the clock and fixing problems of the past: not exactly on Barry's agenda. Never had been.

"Uncle Barry," the one who wore the Peterson Elementary shirt said in a gravelly tone, "we are waiting. Got any more eggs with toys on one side and candy on the other?"

Barry's nose smelled the decay and rot of the dead children. He did not reply.

"I think, Uncle Barry, you are holding out." Peterson Elementary twisted his head to one of the others, the neck bone popping. "Don't you think so, Jeffery?"

A dead kid stepped forward, his clothes were ripped and torn hanging, off his decaying body. "Yep. He's holdin' out on us. We want our candy and toys, Uncle Barry. Please?"

"I—I gave them to you. Long time ago," Barry mumbled in a terrified voice.

189

"*Did* you?" a voice spoke out of the dark. A dead girl walked over, joining the two boys. "I don't think I ever got one. You told me if I went with you to your house you would give me a whole box of 'em."

"Yeah!"

"Yep."

Both boys said.

"Don't hold out on us, Uncle," the girl said. "You know you've gotta follow through."

"I—I know I gave each of you an egg!" Barry snapped. "I know I did."

"Nuh-uh!" Another dead child materialized out of the dark, holding a large knife. "Don't you lie, Uncle. Ain't nice!" The child ran his finger along the edge of the blade.

"Yeah," the girl added.

"Look, you kids have already got your eggs!" Barry shouted. "Leave me alone!" Peterson Elementary threw his head back and laughed. "Leave you alone? Leave you alone? You told us to *leave you alone?* Hey, Jeffery," he nudged the kid with his shoulder, "get a load-ah-this guy! He says he wants to be left alone."

Jeffery laughed. The others joined him.

"Why would we want to do that? Huh?"

Barry didn't respond.

"Speak up! Why on earth would we want to do that, Uncle Barry? You didn't do that for us, did you?"

A spark of frustration filled Barry. "Now, look, you kids, you get the hell outta my pla—"

"NO1" the boy's words bounced off the walls. The flames in the fireplace grew and Barry drew back, pressing his head against the chair's cushion. "*You* look, Uncle Barry. You invaded our world long ago." Barry held his breath, not wanting to smell the protruding stench. "See? You took it all away. You are the reason why we exist in the world of the dead!" Peterson stuck his face in Barry's and whispered: "You took away the life we could have had. I could have been a policeman. Jeffery could have been a cook. Linda could have been a nurse. Johnny could have been a doctor." The one with the blade sidestepped in view. "Bobby could have been a fireman. But, not now." Peterson stood back, and then turned toward the fire.

Barry blew out air.

"We coulda *been* somebody, Uncle Barry. We could have grown up and been somebody. You took it all away. Came into our peaceful world and smashed it like a wrecking ball." He slammed his fist on the mantel over the fireplace and the flames grew for the second time. He gazed at the picture of Barry's mom. "Something, wasn't she? A good mother, right?"

Barry did not want to speak. Terror washed over his body. And, he had to pee.

"She showed you how to live, right? Brought you up right. Took you under her wing. Gave you love. Took you into her bed and—"

"Shut up! I don't want to hear it!" Barry snapped, holding his hands over his ears.

"Oh, but you *do!* You want to hear it!" The boy ran over and two pieces of sandpaper pulled Barry's hands away. "You want to hear it! You want to feel the pain!" Sandpaper burrowed into Barry's skin until the bones snapped.

Barry cried out. His bowels let go.

"We want to take what life you have! We want to watch you bleed for us. Will you, Uncle Barry? Will you bleed for us?"

"Pretty please?" the girl said.

"And don't forget the candy and toys," the one with the knife said, stepping forward, plunging the knife into Barry's gut.

Small hands of each dead child reached inside Barry and pulled his intestines out, his liver, and snapped a rib bone free as they dug and dug. Barry screamed. Cords stuck out of his neck.

"Lookee there, I got a toy to play with!" the boy with the knife fingered two rib bones, sticking them atop his head. "Ha! Look at me! I'm a charging bull!" He bent down and ran around the room in circles.

The girl held up a liver and said: "Anyone want liver and onions for dinner?"

"Yuk!" one of the kids said.

"Give me that knife," Peterson Elementary said, "I wanna see what else we got in there." Grabbing the knife, he switched the blade's direction, the sharp end up, and sliced Barry completely open. Warm blood washed on both of the pedophile's legs.

Barry grew cold.

The point of the knife found Barry's eyes, plucking them out one by one, as his throat contracted, gasped.

"Not a very good idea to gurgle blood, Uncle Barry," the girl said. "Gotta spit and repeat."

Barry's soul drifted out of his body, watching overhead as the children flayed his corpse. The white light did not arrive for Barry, no long tunnel to pull him upward; only a darkness where hundreds of small child-sized hands reached out and pulled him downward into the depths of Hell.

The dead children, finished with their masterpiece, wearing glistening remains of Barry, were very happy. Now, they could rest. Their souls could finally be satisfied and drift into a ghostly world called the Stygian Wake. They would no longer haunt the woods. They would no longer have to scream for help to anyone who entered the woods, knowing the living could never hear them, always ignored.

But Barry had been different. He'd been given the special talent to hear the children whom he murdered.

Together, the children dragged the mutilated corpse of Barry outside into the woods and stood back as a thunderclap shrieked the sky, shaking leaves from the trees. A bright orb materialized, lights speared Barry's corpse. There was a *whirr* and a *clank* as a large mechanical claw reached out, plucking the murdering pedophile from the ground, stuffing him inside the light. Another thunderclap, and the orb rocketed into the sky, disappeared.

While the tractor trailer displaying BAILEY'S FINEST CHEW IN THE TERRITORY! NOW IN WINTERGREEN AND WATERMELON FLAVORS roared past in front of Barry's house and headed in the direction of downtown.

Chapter 38

One lady sat in the pew praying for her dead son who had died long ago from pneumonia. Very young, very fragile. The doctors could only do so much at County General. She knew they had done their best, and did not blame them for his passing. The sickness came on one night and did not let up until it murdered her son four days later. His body could not fight it off. His temperature had started at one hundred, slowly rising to a hundred and two over the course of the days, until, finally, at a hundred and five, it fried his brain.

She had lost her husband to cancer three years prior, and now prayed for him as well. She knew God took care of both her son and her husband. They were definitely in a better place.

Her old eyes found Jesus on the cross, lights beneath Him accenting the two stakes in his palms and the one through his feet. His head lolled to the side with his expression showing pain.

The lady whispered a prayer. A tear ran down her cheek. She picked up her purse and slid out of the pew, stopped.

The doors were closed and the holy water sat in a fountain with the statue of Mother Mary standing over it. Her hands were clasped together and her head hung forward, praying. To the side stood a child.

"Mommy," the voice crackled.

"Danny?"

"It's me, Mommy. I've come home."

"D—Danny?" Her voice cracked, tears filled her eyes. "Is it really you?" She gasped. *How could her boy be here?*

"I've missed you, mommy. I wanna come home."

The lady stood there as Danny walked to her, leaving a path of grave dirt, a smile across his face, stretching what flesh had not yet decayed and fallen off.

The mother held out her arms to embrace her son as he ran to her. A pungent odor, she continued to squeeze him tight. "I—I missed you so much, Danny," she sobbed. "I'm so sorry! I'm so sorry I hit you! I'm so sorry I mistreated you! I have changed since your death! The doc has me on better meds. Can you ever forgive me?"

"Sure, mommy."

As the statue of Jesus watched, Danny raised the blade, brought it down into his mother's back, over and over, until the blood splattered the nearby pews.

In the end, the boy looked up at the Savior, and smiled.

Chapter 39

People in the lobby at the ER sat in the chairs waiting to be called back. The backup generator made the lights dim from time to time. Only two children, each with the flu, sat there with their parents. The rest were adults. Some sick, some in the need of stitches.

A woman who with a migraine lifted her eyes, barely, and saw the child stroll in. He wobbled, almost fell, and caught himself. His hands covered his face, his head hung forward. Though the pain of the migraine had crashed into her temples, the vise clamping down and squeezing, had taken five.

At times it would happen, returning with vengeance.

The woman couldn't believe what she saw. A child covered in blood, wandering aimlessly, not one person noticing him. She didn't even notice the receptionist open her window, head bent, writing something. So, she stood up. A sharp wave of pain raked across her forehead and she almost had to sit back down. But didn't. She stumbled over to the child. Heads turned as she passed, now observing the lonely child.

"Honey? Wh—," her eyes squeezed shut, feeling a sharper pain, "What happened?" She bent down, trying to see his face.

"What happened to him?" a voice said.

The lady turned to see a tall guy slowly standing. Brows raised, he whipped his head to the side: "Hey, this kid needs help! Got a problem out here!"

A window slid back and an older woman's face appeared, flavored with a disgusted look. "What's wrong? What do you all need? We are working as hard as and fast as we c—"

"There's a child out here needing more help than us!" the guy spat. Glancing at the other who were waiting to be seen, they did not counter. "Look! Looks like the kid has been in a wreck."

The old face peered out of the window. And her eyes widened. "Oh, Lord!" Disappearing from view her voice echoed: "Donny! We've got a problem out front!"

The double doors leading back to the ER rooms flew open and three nurses ran out. The woman with the migraine saw this and turned back to the boy. He stood there, head hung low, sobbing.

"Shhh." It's gonna be okay, these nice people are gonna help you. What's your name?" She heard footsteps rush up behind her and when the boy dropped his hands, she wished he hadn't asked. As much pain as her headache induced, she first thought she was having a hallucination. The kid looked as if he had crawled from a grave.

"Hewoh, pretty lady!" the boy cackled. "Wanna have some fun?"

Cold air whisked through the lobby and the concerned woman could have sworn she saw a shadow crawl over the wall and slip down a hallway toward the front of the hospital. The nurses stopped in their tracks.

"Son," a male nurse said, "what happened to you?"

"Oh, me?" The boy giggled. "Ain't nuffin' wrong with me. You're the ones who'll have to seek some treatment for your inflictions. And what a better place to be when you receive them!"

The nurse frowned. "Do what?"

One of the children who sat with his mother gazed at her, opened wide and puked, splashing her with black blood. The kid stood up and threw punches into her the face. The other kid clambered atop his father and bit down, ripped open the guy's cheek.

The wave of the migraine came back for another approach, a kamikaze attack, emanating ripples of pain. She lost her balance, fell to the floor, holding onto her head. Tears streamed from her eyes.

The world around her twisted. Shouts were heard. Screaming bounced off the walls. The blood covered child attacked the nurses, stabbing them with a large ice pick. Crimson spotted their white uniforms.

While the two sick children slowly murdered their parents, the boy who had slaughtered the nurses attacked others. The woman with the migraine made a staggering run for the exit. Once the glass doors slid open a line of children stood there like soldiers. They all pulled their lips back in a grin when they saw her and stepped forward.

She bolted back inside the hospital.

She ran through the lobby and found the stairwell taking the steps in twos and threes, not really aware where to go. She ran and ran and ran and ran. Passing the first floor, the second floor, the third, the fourth, the fifth, and before she knew it, arrived on the sixth. A wave of pain from the migraine stopped her in her tracks and she crashed, holding onto her head. This time the pain intensified, not giving her a break. Too bad she couldn't cut her head off. Shear the damn thing off her shoulders. Bile crawled up her throat, bringing waves of nausea, forcing it out because her salad she had ate for lunch had left her stomach an hour go. Her vision blurred, the lights in the stairwell brightened, shoving more unforgiving pain in her eye sockets.

Slowly, she managed to crawl up the steps to the very next floor, pushing open the door with her hand, and rolling face up on the floor, squinted at the bright lights. She rolled over. The hallway lay empty. Pictures of pink and blue elephants holding balloons, a mother duck and her little ducks following behind her, clowns with big feet and large, round noses and smiles under their noses, patterned the walls.

Footsteps. A head blocked out the light. Her vision blurred. She told the person something horrifying was going on downstairs. Someone needed to get down there fast. Call the police. Do something.

The figure said he knew that. Everything was going to be okay. She was safe. Where did she hurt? He could get her some medication for the pain. He would be happy to help her because, hey, this is the place to make people feel all the much better, right?

She agreed, not paying close attention to the voice, telling her helper her head was killing her.

The voice said no problem. His head disappeared, bringing the light back down to splash her face, a form of radiation melting her flesh. She heard footsteps walked away while the vise squeezed. She wondered where the voice went, hoping the person would not be gone very long. She prayed they wouldn't.

Before long the voice returned and informed her to lie very still, they were going to take care of her head.

Well, good. Maybe they'll move her into a room and into a bed. The thought of a syringe full of feel-better serum to take the pain away would be a relief.

Small hands touched her. Before she asked if they were going to move her into bed another pain begun.

Cold metal sliced and twisted and dug into her neck. Her senses switched gears, the attack of the migraine snuggled up with new pain. Her neurotransmitters delved into the land of confusion. Which reaction was worse: the terror of the migraine, or the terror of her new pain?

Her neurotransmitters decided to deliver both terrors in unison.

She wanted to scream, she wanted to call out for help, though, could only lie there and moan and do nothing as the blade sawed through the flesh and bone.

Back and forth, forth and back, back and forth.

Afterwards a small hand reached down and grabbed the leaking head by its hair and held it up in front of its ash-gray face.

The three naked infants giggled. They tossed it to one another, playing a game of hot potato. Later, they decided to cut into the woman's body and see how slippery her organs were to hold onto.

A new game.

A squishy heart with valves, much like nipples; a moist lung thin, bereft of oxygen; a liver, thick and small enough to resemble a cow's tongue; all a list of organs inside a flesh-covered toy box. Rooted into, pulled free, passed around, tossed to each other, and played with until the organs withered and became rotten.

And as they cut into the woman's bleeding corpse, the sign over their heads said: "Maternity Ward".

Chapter 40

Patty's scream lodged in her throat, a huge lump of mucus. Wouldn't release, clamped down by more fear than what her body could take. Here a small child stood, covered in blood, holding the corpse of a baby in its hand with a tail in the other.

No. Not a tail, an umbilical cord.

"Whassup, Patty?"

She didn't respond. Something stung her finger, bringing her back to reality. She twitched and the piece of glass she had picked up fell back down to the floor. Blood seeped from a small slit in her fingertip.

"Got any milk and cookies? Me and my brother want some." The child dragged the tiny corpse, leaving a light red smear on the floor, and climbed on a bar stool, flipping his brother up on the bar using the umbilical cord.

Patty backed against the register on the counter behind her. Her eyes found the dead baby. Its face had been torn off, possibly from scraping the ground. Three of its fingers were gone. Ashen-grey colored the child's face.

Why did he look like that?

Her brain served no response.

"So," the child's voice became hoarse, "how 'bout that milk and cookie? I like oatmeal and raisin." He drummed his little fingers. "My bro here likes the same. Right, bro?" He stuck the dead baby's face close to his ear. "Yup. He says he likes the same." Hollow eyes, oozing black, ran down his cheeks, glared at her.

Patty stood frozen. "Wh-What happened to you, kid?"

"Happened? Oh, all this?" He laughed, waving a hand in front of his face. "Well, Patty, me and my friends have been reborn."

"Reborn?" she whispered.

"Yeah. Reborn. You don't have to whisper it, Patty. You can say it out loud. Most people around here know it already. The words won't bite ya or anything." He paused, touched a finger to his lips. "I might though. Guess you'll know soon enough."

Patty swallowed.

"See, the world is changing. It is shifting forward to a better place, Patty. And, already, Scooter has joined the movement. He had trouble choosing his own path." He leaned forward and lowered his voice. "But Eddie chose it for him." He giggled.

"Eddie?"

"Oh, you, know, *Eddie.* Son of Wendy. Stepson of Shro?"

Speechless. Had this kid —or whatever sat here —help kill her Scooter? Her heart sank. Worry filled her expression. Her eyes filled up with tears.

"Now, I know what your thinkin', Patty," he paused, "the answer is no. I didn't help Eddie kill Scooter. Eddie done it all by himself. "He cleared his throat and sighed. "Anyway, how about a large glass of milk and cookie? My throat's dry."

"We don't serve milk here." She whispered.

"What? Can't hear ya?" the child cupped a hand over his ear.

"W—We don't serve it here. You need to leave."

"Leave? We just got here." He pointed to the corpse. "Ain't that right, bro? You want some cookies and milk, don't ya?"

The baby said nothing.

"Geez! Can't get a rise outta him, can I? Useless as making a dead bird fly. I know he wants a cookie, too. He's juss bein' quiet."

Patty sidestepped, thinking the backdoor wasn't far away.

The child stared at her, his face solid as a rock.

Seconds passed.

"Well?" he snapped. "We're waiting Patty."

Patty bolted toward the back and heard the kid say, "Come back here! You ain't supposed to leave! We want our cookies and milk!"

She passed the pool tables, passed the juke box that only played oldies —nothing new because Scooter didn't take to the new music —and ran out the backdoor to confront two more children.

"Hey there, Patty!" They waved. "I came here for cookies and milk. Got any?"

Patty ran back inside and bumped into the side of one of the pool tables, tripped, and fell on her shoulder. Holding her aching shoulder, something cold and clammy touch her cheek.

Matthew stood above her, his brother lying by Patty's face, a close eyeshot of the dead baby. Her throat contracted and she let loose a horrified scream.

"Shhh! Now, now, everything's going to be the much...more... *better!*" the last word Matthew said brought the pain of a cold blade plunging into her stomach and ripping her open. Warm blood leaked out onto the thin carpet, staining it.

Through Patty's guttural shrieks one of the other kids had joined in, kneeling to work his own blade into her flesh, slicing through her jeans, making a jagged C-section cut, soon connecting with the shaved slit between her legs.

Intestines squirmed out on the floor. Long, glistening red worms. When death did arrive, and Patty's soul left her corpse, a hand grabbed hers, a voice softly expressing how much he loved her and was sorry for the way things ended.

The pain of the sadistic mutilations gone, Patty floated into the white light.

Chapter 41

Tray and the survivors of Hampshire pulled in front of the sheriff's office, a large brick building built in the seventies with a flat roof. Two concrete columns held up an overhang with double glass doors lying directly below. No lights blazed through the windows. Not even the street lights displayed light along the street. Three police cars sat out front.

A malodorous smell of human decay drifted in the broken windows of Tray's semi.

Tray gagged. "Nastier than a dead skunk flattened on the road on a hot August day!"

Shro screwed his face up in disgust, covered it with his hand.

Wendy held her hand over mouth, hoping not to vomit, while Martha followed suit.

"Doesn't look to be anyone at home," Shro said, slipping out of the truck behind Wendy, gazing at the place. "'Closed up like this entire town. Sure we wanna do this? Why don't we go and try Deputy Point or somthin'?"

"No," Wendy said. "We need to see if there is a cop around here in town. The ones in Deputy Point don't have any jurisdiction here in Hampshire. They wouldn't be able to help us."

"Cops aren't gonna be much help, Wendy," Tray said. "They're probably all dead. The looks of that station should prove the point."

"What do we do, then?"

"We'll need more guns. More ammo. Maybe the police station still has weapons."

"You still have your pistol?"

"Nope. Lost it back there. Got bullets though."

Martha twisted her head to the side. "The air is definitely cooler. Feel it?"

"Yeah. I do," Tray replied. "Wind has picked up. Damn odor hanging around pretty thick here. Maybe we'll get lucky and the wind'll carry it off." He rubbed his nose.

"Not this kinda wind," Martha said as an unsettled feeling uncoiled inside her gut.

"What the hell was that thing we drove through?" Wendy asked.

"Don't know," Tray responded.

Martha said. "It was the shape of the beast out of the Book of Revelations."

"Beast?" Shro asked.

"The beast. The one who dwells below. The one called Lucifer, in the flesh."

Shro shuddered. "Are you serious? Next thing you'll tell me it could be the—"

"End of the world."

Shro's face blanched. Unimaginable scenes of destruction flashed in front of his eyes of fire: impaled, burning bodies, a dude with a pitchfork and two horns on his head.

"Wonder if those cruisers have any shotguns in them?" Tray said.

"Need to check, but if we are going into that station to find any guns," Martha said, "we need to be damn careful."

Wendy walked over to one of the cruisers, found the door unlocked, bent down, reached inside, found a shotgun.

"Is it loaded?" Martha asked.

Wendy hadn't shot a gun for some time. Even Shro didn't know she had. But, she knew how to handle the weapon. She opened the shotgun with the barrel angled down, exposing the breech ends, and checked for the ammo. "It's loaded." She bent down and crawled into the cruiser further, coming back with a handful of shotgun shells. "Shro. Check the other car."

"Sure." Surprised Wendy knew how to carry a gun, check it for ammo, Shro didn't inquire about it. Actually, he was happy she knew that much. This damnation they were in needed as many people who knew how to fire a gun. He checked the other car and didn't come up empty handed, either, finding a shotgun and a Billy club. "Bonus! Check it out! This'll help!"

Tray chuckled. He checked the last cruiser, found both doors locked. "Gimme that club, Shro."

Shro handed it to him. "Stand back." Tray reared back, smashing the side window. Carefully reaching in, he unlocked the door, and in no time held another shotgun in hand. He reached in again and came back with a flashlight.

Wendy smiled. "Good thinking." She walked over to the same car where she found her gun and located a flashlight too.

"Surprised the other two cars weren't locked," Tray said. "You'd think it was common sense leaving your police cruiser locked."

"True," Martha said, "but good for us, not having to smash two windows. Nothing bad has ever happened in all the years I've lived in this small, country town. Never had to worry about much, until now."

"Things have changed. Where I was born we had to keep our doors locked. I'm from a big city. Once we moved out in the country, didn't have to worry about burglary. My Pa always said the country was much better, cleaner air and such, you know?"

"Not anymore," Shro said. "Place is turned upside down. Madness, like some horror flick."

The other three agreed.

"Guess I'll have to get me a gun inside," Martha said, looking to see if there might be another police cruiser parked around the corner.

"You can stay behind if you want," Tray said.

"Oh, no. I think I've earned my stripes after what I went through."

"Martha can use a shotgun pretty damn well, man," Shro said.

"No kiddin'?" Tray smiled and looked at Martha.

"Yep," Martha said. "My late husband, Frank, showed me how a long time ago."

"Good. We'll get you a firearm inside, if we find one. Stay behind us. If something jumps out at us, one of us will blow 'em apart."

"Sounds like a plan."

"We all ready to see what's inside?" Wendy asked. Somehow, she felt stronger now, even though her Eddie had gone. Her sadness for his — she didn't want to think or say it— death drove her forward. Whatever evil attacked Hampshire, she wanted it gone. She wished it could be normal again. She wished her Eddie could be a normal kid again.

A voice deep down inside told her he never would.

They cautiously stepped up to the doors. Tray led the way.

Chapter 42

Nancy heard the rumble of a vehicle pull up outside and stop. Relief washed over her. She would be saved – unless the driver doesn't know the maniac children were running around in the police station. Nancy would have to warn them.

But how? Could she shout or scream, and be heard all the way down here in the basement?

And, dammit, the window was too high for her to look out!

She hadn't heard a peep out of the kids, which unnerved her.

What were they up too? Had they worn themselves out?

Kids did wear out. Eventually. Her niece finally crashed when she babysat her last week. Come to think of it, Nancy remembered how worn out *she* was after she took her to the park.

How can those kids have so much energy?

She sighed. The craving for nicotine had been pestering her for the past few minutes. It'd be nice for a smoke.

A door closed, followed by another. A few minutes more and two more were heard. She wondered if more than one person was out there. That would be a blessing! It may take more than one person to help her.

"Nancy." A whisper slipped out of the dark, jerking her away from her thoughts of hope, diminishing them. "We have company. You be a good girl, okay? Don't worry, we're gonna break you out and have some fun later. Right now, we're gonna get warmed up."

As if they hadn't already!

Footsteps across the floor, footsteps climbing the stairs.

Nancy wondered if they had been sitting on the other side of the bars all along, there in the darkness, listening to her movements, hearing her breathe.

Giggling drifted down from above, haunting the dark.

***

The stench of the dead smacked the quartet as they stepped inside. Covering their nose and mouth, they did not venture further. Tray illuminated the room with his flashlight, revealing a gruesome scenery. Shoving back more darkness, Wendy's flashlight beam brought a cold, nauseous feeling crawling inside her stomach.

"Jesus in Heaven," Martha whispered.

The dead were unrecognizable. Each body had been drained of blood and organs and displayed, draped over desks. The eyes had been removed, mouths hung ajar.

"Those damn kids," Wendy said. "They mutilated these people. No telling whether they had been alive, or after they were already dead."

Martha half-smiled at him. "We can only pray they were dead when those kids did this."

Tray nodded. "Let's have a look around and see if we can find any more guns. Try not to step in the blood."

"Too late," Shro said, leaving an imprint as he stepped to the side.

Wendy sidestepped between a desk and a wall. The face of a deflated corpse gazed at her. Wendy could tell it had been a woman. Repulsed, she tore her eyes away. She pressed the flashlight against the long barrel of the shotgun with her left hand, while her right enabled the trigger. If she saw movement, she'd be ready to shoot.

Shro mimicked Wendy, holding his flashlight against his own shotgun barrel.

Tray motioned for Martha to stay behind him, while he followed suit behind Wendy and Shro. He swung his flashlight's beam, revealing dried blood all over the walls. He mouthed the words, "Well, piss on me".

"You sure you want to explore this place, Wendy?" Shro asked from behind her. "Those folks back there are probably the cops. They may *all* be dead, you know."

"We need more firearms, Shro. I don't have any faith in anyone at all being alive in this place."

"You're right, Wendy," Tray agreed. "We need the firepower. We all know this night ain't over yet."

"Amen to that," Martha added. "We may need to pray for our souls. Do each of you all believe in God?"

They all said yes. Martha opened her mouth to say a small prayer as they stepped into a long hallway.

A child's voice spoke out of the dark.

"Hello there! Ready to join the party?" the voice echoed. "There's gonna be prizes!"

"A slightly used police badge to the first who can find me," another voice chimed in.

"How about a policeman's nose? Used correctly you could sure use it to pick up the scent of a murderer." Laughter.

Wendy shone her flashlight down the hall, coming back with nothing except closed doors lined on both side. She wondered if the children were hiding out in them.

"Wendy, are you still sure about this?" Shro asked.

"Let's see if we can locate any more guns and get the hell outta here. Right Tray?"

"Yep. Get what we need and get the hell out," Tray said.

"Help! Anyone up there?" The voice echoed in the hall.

"Who the hell is that?" Tray asked.

"Sounds like it's a woman's. Not one of those kids," Shro said.

"Anyone up there? Somebody please get me out of here!"

"Think it's a trick?" Wendy said.

"Only one way to find out," Martha said.

The group moved forward, keeping a close eye in front, to the side, and behind them. Pictures of officers hung on the walls and a large picture of a beach hung crooked.

"Anyone there? Please! I'm trapped down here in a cell."

"There's a door, right there," Shro flashed his light, "where the holding cells are."

Wendy looked over her shoulder.

"Don't ask. I was down there once."

"Why?"

Shro sighed. "It was when, uh, I got into a fight at Scooter's."

"You did *what?*"

"Sorry." He scratched the back of his head. "Remember when I said I got too drunk to drive and Scooter said I could stay at the bar?"

"Yeah, I think I remember." Wendy thought it sounded a little odd at the time, instead of Scooter offering to drive him home. "I wasn't too happy about it."

"I know. Scooter had me arrested."

"Scooter? Your buddy had you arrested?"

"Yep."

"Probably good for you, then."

Shro winced, as if slapped.

Wendy shook her head. "Shro, you never cease to amaze me sometimes."

"Now wait a minu–"

"Is anyone up there? I need help!"

The words brought back present time.

Wendy called out: "Are you okay? Are you hurt?"

A short pause. "I'm okay. Good to hear you. You need to watch out for those kids. They've already killed everyone else here."

"Thought so. Are you safe?" Wendy asked.

"Safer than you. I'm behind bars."

Wendy wondered if the woman *was* safer behind bars. Made sense. Could the kids be tricking them?

Only one way to find out.

"We're coming down," Wendy informed.

"We're? There's more than one of you?"

"Yeah. Four."

"Good! But be careful, those kids were down here with me until they heard your vehicle pull up. No telling where they are now."

Footsteps behind the party.

Tray trained his gun and his light down the hall. Nothing stirred.

"Ready to go down?" Wendy asked all.

"Sure," Shro said, though his tone sounded shaky.

"Might as well. We need to save as many souls as we can." Martha said, while Tray nodded.

Wendy used her flashlight, cutting through the dark path on the way down. Tray brought up the rear, his back against the wall, his gun and flashlight pointed at anything attempting to slip out of the dark.

Child or rat.

"Where are you?" Wendy flashed her light as she stepped off the last step. Three jail cells ran along one side of the room.

"The last cell. I locked myself in." A thin hand stuck through the bars and waved.

Wendy hurried over. The woman looked familiar. Probably a customer at the Truck Stop at one time or another. "Where's the key to the lock?"

"It's broke. It snapped off when I ran in here."

"Snapped off?" Shro came into view.

"Yeah. Those kids chased me down here and when I slammed the cell shut, I had the key still in the slot. I accidently snapped it off."

Shro looked at it. Saw the broken stub of the key in the hole. "How are we gonna get this thing open?"

"Watch out a sec, young man," Martha grabbed the shotgun out of his hands and said, "Hold your ears everyone. Ma'am, please get against the wall."

The gun blast reverberated down the passage, vibrated the bones under their skin. Now the cell door lay ajar.

"Damn, that was loud!" Shro said.

"Told ya to keep your hands over your ears." Martha turned to Shro. The others had done what she said, while Shro's ears rang. "Come on, hon, let's get you outta here."

The woman stepped out of the cell. "Thanks ..?"

"Martha. That's Shro, We—."

"Nancy." She pointed to herself. "Can we all get out of here, worry with introductions later? I need to leave this miserable place."

"Sure," Shro said.

"Are there any more guns around?" Wendy asked.

The woman thought for a minute. "Upstairs in one of the rooms."

"Know which one?"

"Yeah."

"We need to collect a few."

They climbed out of the basement. Wendy's flashlight picked out four figures. Each one a rat.

Nancy gasped. *First there had been savage children, now giant rats?*

"Lookee, lookee, lookee here. You saved poor little Nancy," one snarled, its beady eyes glaring at a terrified Nancy.

"How about yourselves? Can you save your own skin?" another

said.

One of the rats took a step forward, sniffed the air. "Mmmmm. I smell fresh blood."

"Nothin' matches the sweet smell of human flesh."

Wendy held the shotgun at her waist. "Nancy? Which door has the guns in it?"

"The last one on the right."

"Great! Right smack where those creatures are standin'." Shro shook his head.

"Ain't nothin' easy now, son," Tray raised his gun. "We've been doomed at the start of this horror. Raise that gun and get ready to blast your way to the guns and out of this place."

Shro took aim.

The rats started off, claws spread wide.

Wendy fired and blew one of them back, knocking the one into another.

Tray fired and the face of a rat went flying, splattering blood, whiskers, part of a black nose, brains and rat flesh on the wall.

Shro blew off a rat's claw. It squealed while a geyser of blood squirted out of the stump. But it didn't stop, running forward, tackling Shro and taking Tray as well.

Their guns slipped from their grip, slid across the floor.

Nancy backed away, watching the rat, which had crashed the floor, rise, growl, and attack.

Martha snatched up a gun, steadied herself, and fired.

The rat's head exploded, the body crashed into the wall.

Martha was shocked the figure hadn't risen back up. *Is that how they are finally killed?*

Shro and Tray managed to get away from the rat, though, unfortunately, not away from a scrape of its claws.

Wendy pulled the trigger and blew half the creature's face off. It stumbled, fell face-first and lay still. The beam of her flashlight revealed the horrible, sickening remains of the rats in sprawled out on the floor.

"I can't believe we killed them," Martha said, shocked. "When I had to shoot Penny she had some sort of protected skin over her."

"Yeah," Tray agreed, his face brightened. "Some cocoon or protective shield before they evolved into a rat."

"There's the room where the guns are," Nancy pointed.

Wendy shone her flashlight and tried opening the door. Locked. She used the butt of her gun to knock off the doorknob. Lifting the barrel of her gun, she entered inside.

"I found some guns."

The small party hurried into the room and saw a glass cabinet full of rifles and shotguns. Lockers and two long benches filled the rest of the room.

"Found a pot of gold, huh?" Tray said.

"Yep." Wendy used the butt of her gun again, smashing the glass. She ran the barrel along the lip of the window, chipping away glass shards. "Let's get what we need."

They took turns rummaging through and pulling free an extra weapon. They grabbed up boxes and boxes of shells.

"Here are a few duffle bags," Shro pointed out, stepping over to the corner of the room, reaching behind the side of a locker.

"Good find. Let's throw the shells and the guns in there," Wendy said.

Nancy picked up a shotgun and frowned.

"Ever shot one before?" Martha asked.

"Not really," Nancy replied. "Never interested in a firearm."

"Here, let me give you a crash course." While she did, the others packed what they could. Shro carried the duffle bag, and started out the door, returning through the room of the slaughtered bodies.

Shro stopped. "Hear that?"

They all listened.

Tray said, "Yeah. Some sort of weird music. None I've ever heard before."

"Look outside," Nancy said and pointed, walking out of the room with Martha.

Rats and children were walking in a long line down the street, passing by Tray's truck, face-forward, not looking at anything else, some dragging corpses of adults in tow; either having the locks of the hair looped around their claws, or their claws hooked into the gaping mouths, pulled back in a silent scream. Some bodies were bloody, some had brittle, crusted up skin where it had been scorched.

"This just keeps gettin' better 'n better," Tray shook his head.

"We need to get out the back door," Wendy said. "Nancy? Where's the back door?" Nancy amazed at the line of savages outside and their dead captives.

"Nancy?"

Nancy looked at Wendy. "Wh-What?"

"The back door. Where is it?"

"We'll have to go back into the hall, hang a left, follow it to the back."

"It's our only chance outta here. Unless it's blocked by those creatures. Go ahead and lead the way, Nancy."

Flashlight beams shoving back more darkness, they followed Nancy to door. Wendy tried to open it, and found it jammed shut.

"Okay," Wendy said. "If we stay in here, we're probably dead. If those creatures outside start pouring in through the front doors we'll be able to hold them off."

"Don't think so either, Wendy," Tray said. "No telling how many are walkin' the streets."

"So, what do we do?" Shro asked.

Wendy pondered. "I have an idea. I'll go check out why the door is blocked. Maybe I'll be able to open it so we can all get away from here."

"That's suicide," Tray said. "That's not a good idea."

"Tray, there's no sense in all of us exiting through the front door while those creatures are out there in the street. If only one of us goes, it might be quicker than all of us in a long line slipping outside at once."

Tray frowned.

"Anyways, I'm a little healthier than you guys. I've been a runner for about a year."

"Point taken," Tray sighed. "But I'd feel best if you didn't go out there by yourself." He turned to Shro. "Right?"

"Um…yeah, I guess." Shro said.

"Please tell me you don't approve of your wife doing this by yourself?"

"Uh…no. Hell no!" Shro tried to sound serious. "I'll go with you, Wendy."

"You better. I love you Shro but sometimes …sometimes you can be an idiot."

Shro swallowed.

"Tray's right. I don't need to do this alone, Shro."

"Okay. I'm going with you."

"Our Eddie's dead because of those things outside and whatever the hell is going on here in Hampshire. We all need to get out of this building and get out of town."

Each one agreed with her.

"I guess it's a safe bet we may be the only survivors, huh?" Martha asked.

"If a bull frog don't eat flies, no," Tray replied. "But we know better than that. Right?"

Martha nodded. Leaving her hometown didn't set well with her. Though, dealing with those creatures gave her the impetus to get the hell out and don't look back. Too many memories left behind, here with her Frank. It was the end of the world.

Those demonic kids and rats and their master proved it.

Chapter 43

The entity stood at the end of town, his instrument to his lips.

The wind carried his melodic notes, seeking out the ears of the many children whom the he had acquired by possession, pulling them from the darkness, leaving their killings in their wake. Hordes of demonic children had arrived. Some still of human flesh. Others morphed of fur and fangs and claws. Soon they would all mutate into rats, shedding their cocoons of human flesh, a rebirth toward the shift of the world.

The entity withdrew his instrument and began to speak to them. He explained how happy he had become for what they had done to the people of Woodbury and Hampshire. He explained what The Reckoning had planned for them all, once the actual Shift, the change of the world, had begun moving its steel wheel toward its birthing.

Beady eyes gazed at their master.

The ones who could not see, but could hear, tore away their cocoons of flesh.

Chapter 44

"Keep low to the ground, Shro. We may be able to stay out of sight."

Wendy and Shro cautiously slid out of the front of the police station and crept around the side.

"Huh. Those creatures are stopping for some reason, Wendy," Shro whispered.

Wendy glanced over her shoulder. "Did they see us?"

"No. Don't think so."

"Keep moving!"

Shotguns in hand they curved around the edge of the building and saw where a dumpster had been moved against the back door.

"Easy fix," Shro said, "we can roll it outta the way."

"Should be able to," Wendy said.

Both husband and wife placed their hands on the dumpster and gave it a push. It didn't budge.

"Crap!" Wendy spat.

"Give it another push, Wendy! It should be easier to move than this."

They tried again.

"Damn!" Wendy said.

"Turn around, use your legs. That's it, now *push!*"

The dumpster barely moved.

"Okay. One more time, Wendy," Shro said. "Get set. One, two, three ... *push!*"

It moved two feet, scraped the ground.

"Crap!" Wendy peeked under the dumpster. "The wheels are crushed underneath!"

"What?" Shro looked. "Son of a bitch!"

"It's gonna take a vehicle to push it out of the way, Shro."

"Maybe Tray can get his truck back here." Shro wiped his forehead.

Wendy scanned the alley. "Looks too tight to try and fit it back here. We could try and get a cop car and ram this thing."

Shro nodded.

"Let's get back and tell the others." Wendy led the way back, stopped when there were shotgun blasts.

She glanced back at Shro, wide-eyed. Both raced around the front and Shro took notice to the street being empty, then noticed three dead rats lying in front of the doors, gunshot wounds in their face and chests.

Another shotgun blast rang from inside, bouncing off the buildings in the square.

"We need to help them!" Wendy stepped inside the building. Two rats faced her. She pulled the trigger. A craniums blew apart. Fur and blood splattered the walls.

Shro followed her lead, blasting the other rat.

A scream echoed out of the hallway.

"Sounds like Nancy!" Wendy said. "We need to get to them!" Two steps forward rats exited the hall through the doorway and attacked Wendy and Shro.

A quick reload and more gunfire brought bodies crashing to the ground.

A small child slipped between two rats wielding a cleaver.

Shro mowed her down.

Wendy quickly fed more shells into the breach and blew apart a rat. If Shro hadn't been there the girl's mouth would be on the front of her throat, chewing away.

Two children ran at Shro as he fumbled to feed more shells in the gun. Nearly tackled, Wendy came to his rescue, catching both monsters blindsided with her shot, making them stumble and fall.

Another blast from a shotgun, this in the hallway, and another scream.

Nancy's.

More rats appeared, as if someone had opened a cage.

"They're trapped!" Wendy said, blasting away another creature.

"We need to save them!" Shro shouted.

"I don't know if we can, Shro. They may be doomed!"

***

Tray had been on guard when Shro and Wendy slipped outside, but it didn't take long for one of the rats to pass by and notice the door close. It saw Shro and Wendy leave and instead of following them, gazed at the police station.

The rat dropped the corpse it held and crashed through the door.

More rats followed suit, seeking flesh and blood.

Tray blasted the first creature outside. "Get down the hall!"

"I'm not leaving you by yourself. " Martha ducked behind a desk, took aim, blasted the second rat.

Nancy cowered down beside her and laid down her weapon.

"Pick up that firearm, child!" Martha snapped. "It's no good lying there on the floor!"

"I—I—I don't know if I ca—"

"Yes you can! Pick it up and shoot it!"

After those words a third rat burst through. Tray took aim and blew the rat backward. "Damn varmint!" he spat.

Nancy screamed.

Bodies of children and rats pushed their way inside. Martha grabbed Nancy and dragged her out of the room two seconds before three rats rushed Tray, slamming him to the hard floor. The rats clawed into him.

Martha poked the barrel of her shotgun into the room and fired.

The blast opened up fresh wounds on two of the rats on top of Tray. A large piece of his face stuck inside one of the rat's maw.

Tray's body jerked and twitched and bled.

Martha took aim again and fired, blowing a hole in the third rat's head, ending its feeding.

More bodies shoved their way through the front door.

Nancy crouched down holding her hands over her head.

"Get up and get your ass in gear!" Martha shoved Nancy. "Get your gun and help me!"

Nancy's bottom lip quivered. "I can't. I CAN'T!"

Dammit! This girl has frozen up on me! She's in shock!

A female child hopped up on one of the desks closest to the doorway. She hissed, took a leap, and tackled Martha. Both hands around her throat. Martha's firearm slipped out of her grip.

Nancy watch in horror as the woman tried fighting off the child.

The kid slapped her. Punched her. Seized Martha around the throat again.

Martha couldn't break away. She stretched a hand out to Nancy. The other gripped the child's wrist, one of the two holding her in a vise, shutting off her oxygen. She mouthed "Help…me."

Nancy continued to watch the child strangle Marta. She did not move.

Martha gasped for air.

Nancy get the hell up and fire that gun! Nancy screamed at herself. She rose. Her legs wobbled. *C'mon! Pick up the gun and shoot!*

Martha's eyes rolled back in her head.

Nancy picked up her gun, took aim, fired. The girl flew into the wall, smearing black blood from her wound.

Nancy was knocked against the wall from the gun's kick. Her head took most of the blow, scattering her vision. Slow to rise, pain sheared across the base of Nancy's head. She tried getting up but a rat took a leap off the desk and slammed down on her, snapping her spine. It chewed into the side of Nancy's face, stretching and ripping her skin off.

Martha half rose, giving a push off the floor with her hand, and sucked in oxygen, filling her lungs. Before she could rise a new attacker slammed her back to the floor, snapping her arm. She mustered a cry through her dry lips, peering up at a shrieking rat, its mouth wide open.

***

"Close that side door and look in the front, Shro. See if there are keys in the ignition."

"Not this one," Shro said. "Try the other one, Wendy, while I search the last one."

Wendy knew Tray, Martha and Nancy were doomed. There was no way to save them. So, she told Shro they needed to save themselves.

Wendy slid behind the wheel of the cruiser. Luckily, the keys were stuck in the ignition. "Got the keys to this one, Shro. Jump in!"

"Somebody likes us up there!" Shro slipped in the passenger seat.

"Maybe. Maybe not." Wendy started up the car. She hated to leave the others behind. Were they dead? She so wanted to tear her way through the station with her shotgun blasts, but it would be suicide. "Let's get the hell out of he–"

The hood to the car bent as a rat crashed down.

Wendy threw the car in reverse and mashed the accelerator, running into Tray's truck, knocking the rat sideways, its claws scraping across the hood trying to hold on.

"Damn!" Shro clamped a hand on the back of his neck.

"Sorry."

"Don't worry about me! Hit the gas!"

The tires spun, leaving a long black mark on the road. They sped away while rats and children took chase after them. Before long, the car outdistanced them, losing their shapes from sight.

"Where do you suppose the line of those creatures were going?" Shro asked.

"Hell if I know, Shro. Let's find us a safe spot to go to. I need to rest."

"Where?"

"Wherever we can."

The drove east, away from Hampshire, and through Deputy Point, where the streets were desolate. Nothing stirred or moved. And for once they realized even the night sounds, the insects haunting the dark, did not speak. Silent as the inside of a buried coffin.

Though what remained, unlike Hampshire, were bodies on each side of the streets in the town square, impaled into the soft ground. Some leaned to the side; some were erect. Slumped figures, lifeless, holding left over residue of terror from the pain, across their faces.

As Wendy and Shro drove on they observed a few more small towns, all empty of life except for more impaled bodies, more of the dead on display. No light of any sort danced behind windows of houses. Nor did the street lights shine down with their rays.

They traveled down a long stretch of road and the wind brought a familiar sound inside. As well as the continuing stench of rotted flesh

"Same music again?" Shro asked.

"Yep." Wendy turned the steering wheel and the tires rolled

over a gravel road, delivering them up onto a hill and parked. She informed Shro it may be wise to keep out of sight if more monsters appeared. Stepping away from the car and walking between trees and out on an edge following the music, their horrors returned.

Below, a huge congregation formed.

All rats, no children. The cocoon of flesh had long left their small bodies, exposing their true forms underneath. Hundreds of them stood together in a clearing, a mass of dark soldiers of the apocalypse off to shift the world forward.

The dark silhouette of the entity, Kabul, stood in front of them, playing a tune.

Shro said. "What now?"

Wendy stood beside him. She had no idea. Where would they go? Could they ever outrun these creatures?

Behind them, a limb snapped. When she turned she opened her mouth to warn Shro, but didn't have a chance to deliver it.

Four rats stood there, claws out, beady eyes black as burnt flesh.

Afterward

Delivered in front of the entity, Shro and Wendy stood awaiting trial. They held hands, knowing the inevitable.

The rats all stood close behind them, lined up in row after row. The entity stood in front, not speaking a word to the prisoners, not even playing a tune.

Before either of them could blink, they watched as the entity split in two and morphed into black, eyeless snakes. Both attacked, slithering all over their bodies, consuming their flesh, blood and memories.

Their bodies convulsed. Their eyes popped out of their sockets and their tongues flipped backward, tore free of the small piece of skin underneath, and squirmed down their throats. Their noses collapsed, flattened against their faces. Their heads lolled backward and their teeth broke off and dropped down into the fleshy tunnel of their throats. Their gums bled and leaked out of their mouths. Their clothes fell free, showing their nakedness. Their flesh rippled, withered and became black, flaking off. Finally, two shells of wet, bloody muscle and bone stood there with hollowed out eyes, holes where their noses should be and a gaping tunnels in place of their mouths before their corpses dropped to the ground.

Hovering overhead The Reckoning watched. They nodded their approval of Kabul. He had followed through with his terror. Simple, effective. Ripped open the countryside's flesh, bringing its horror. The entity proceeded further, leading his rats over the entire planet, gathering more victims, feeding on the ones who had matured into adult.

***

They hadn't killed her.

Martha rose from the massacre at the Hampshire police station, bleeding, her arm broken. She winced as she stumbled over to Nancy's sprawled, mutilated body.

The poor woman had no face.

Locating the Browning, she scooped it up.

When the rat slammed into her it caught a severed desk leg, shoved into its side through fur and flesh. She lay there, playing dead under the dying rat while the others paid her nor their colleague any attention, busy searching for more victims to kill.

Eventually, they left the station.

Her face hurt something fierce and her head pounded. No matter, pain would be something she would have to deal with. She could push it away and replace it with the driving force inside of her—one informing her she'd have to take care of this evil entity herself. She doubted Wendy and Shro had gone after the beast. She feared they may be dead.

Leaving the mutilated bodies of her party behind, trying not to look at the scattered remains, she stepped outside. With vengeance on her mind, God as her co-pilot, Martha spoke a prayer to the Almighty above before stumbling down the street armed with the Browning in her good arm.

About the Author

Brick Marlin has been writing since he was a child. From an early age he was exposed to older horror movies. The great ones making their mark in history. He also tackled reading the likes of Stephen King, Clive Barker, Ray Bradbury, Kurt Vonnegut, Dean Koontz, Charles Dickens, Harper Lee, H.G. Wells, etc. Thus, he decided to engage himself and write horror, dark fantasy and dark sci-fi, scaring readers such as his parents, his friends, neighbors, and even leaving a few school teachers scratching their heads wondering if the boy should be committed or not with his gruesome tales of terror. Short story ideas continued to visit. A book idea or two sometimes stopped by for a sit. In 2007 he decided to take a more professional approach with his work. Hence, as a member of the Horror Writers Association, already having nine books published by small presses – this you hold in your hand, constant reader, makes his tenth – nearly thirty short stories published, adding to the few anthologies and collaborations with other authors, Brick Marlin trudges onward, hoping to achieve more creations, wallowing in the brain pans of his characters, giving them the choice whether to twist the knob and enter through the Red Door, or enter through the Blue Door where a group of servo monkey badgers are consuming packages of cinnamon-flavored Pop Rock Candy with a Kung Fu Punch of caffeine.

Check out the following pages
to see more from

 SEVENTH STAR PRESS

All Seventh Star Press titles available in
print and an array of specially priced eBook
formats.

Visit www.seventhstarpress.com for further
information

Connect with Seventh Star Press at
www.seventhstarpress.com
seventhstarpress.blogspot.com
www.facebook.com/seventhstarpress
www.twitter.com/7thstarpress

Transcend Reality!

Shadows Over Somerset from Bob Freeman!

Softcover: 978-1-941706-11-4
eBook: 978-1-941706-12-1

Michael Somers is brought to Cairnwood, an isolated manor in rural Indiana, to sit at the deathbed of a grandfather he never knew existed. He soon finds himself drawn into a strange and esoteric world filled with werewolves, vampires, witches... and a family curse that dates back to fourteenth century Scotland. In the sleepy little town of Somerset, an ancient evil awakens, hungering for blood and vengeance... and if Michael is to survive he must face his inner demons and embrace his family's dark past. Shadows Over Somerset is the first Cairnwood Manor Novel.

Now Available from Seventh Star Press,
the horror stylings of
Michael West!

Trade Paperback ISBN: 9780983740209
eBook ISBN: 9780983740216

Trade Paperback ISBN: 9781937929718
eBook ISBN: 9781937929725

Trade Paperback ISBN: 9781937929954
eBook ISBN:9781937929831

Trade Paperback ISBN: 978-1-937929-18-3
eBook ISBN: 978-1-937929-19-0

16 Tales of the Paranormal and Ghostly from editors Alexander S. Brown and J.L. Mulvihill!

eBook ISBN: 978-1-937929-14-5

Softcover ISBN: 978-1-937929-12-1

From the shadowed realms of the paranormal comes 16 chilling tales that dwell in the South and South West. From 16 authors, learn of haunted homes, buildings, landmarks and roads where restless entities from beyond the grave desire acknowledgement amongst the living. Become acquainted with the aftermath of an eclipse that awakens the dead in a Memphis cemetery, see what horrors dwell in the woods at Hell's Gate, learn the dark secrets of Sidney's Cotton, and dare to travel down Ghost Road. These and many other tales are sure to keep you awake as you are introduced to what makes the South and South West so unique.... History and GHOSTS!!!!! So, sit back, dim the lights and prepare yourself to face the spirits that walk among us.

Now available! A Seventh Star Press Anthology
from editor Michael West!

eBook ISBN: 978-1-937929-69-5

Softcover ISBN: 978-1-937929-60-2

Vampires Don't Sparkle! poses the question: What would
you do if you had unlimited power and eternal life?

Would you...go back to high school? Attend the same classes
year after year, going through the pomp and circumstance
of one graduation after another, until you found the perfect
date to take to prom? Would you...spend your days moping
and brooding, finding your only joy in a game of baseball
on a stormy day? Or would you...do something else?

The authors of this collection have a few ideas; some fanciful,
some humorous, and some as dark as an endless night.

Join us, and discover what it truly means to be "vampyre."

Post-apocalyptic, zombie-infested military thriller from Peter Welmerink!

Softcover ISBN: 978-1-941706-03-9

eBook ISBN: 978-1-941706-02-2

The HURON, a 72-ton heavy transport vehicle and an army of four; tracked, racked and ready to roll, to serve and protect the walled metropolis of Grand Rapids-both her living and her undead. Captain Jacob Billet and his crew patrol the byways, ready for trouble. William Lettner, the North Shore Coalition High Commissioner, has enemies from the mainland to the lakeshore and needs to be covertly transported home after his helicopter is shot down en route to Grand Rapids. He has no love for a city that give unliving civilians the right to survive. Lettner's venomous outbursts assaults Billet and his crew along every mile travelled as they are assigned to safely bring him through the treacherous landscape outside the city back to his hometown. To complete their mission, the HURON and her crew will have to face domesticated zombies and the feral undead; marauders holding strategic chokepoints hostage; barricaded villages fighting for survival, and a group of geneticists who've lost control of one of their monstrous experiments. The crew will need to stay strong and trust one another in order to finish the mission and bring their "precious" cargo home, even knowing, all the while, the terrible deeds Lettner has done. Travelling through West Michigan was never so dangerous. Transport is the first book in the Transport series!

Hellscapes, Volume 1
Venture through the infernal, where angels
fear to tread!

From Stephen Zimmer, a new horror
series set in realms where the inhabitants
experience the ultimate nightmare!
softcover ISBN: 978-1-937929-36-7
eBook ISBN: 978-1-937929-37-4

Paranormal-laced Horror from Crymsyn Hart!

Softcover: 978-1-941706-13-8
eBook: 978-1-941706-14-5

Being a psychic, you would think talking to the dead was a walk in the park. However, it's not always that simple. The hooded specter haunting me is one I've been dreaming about since I was a kid. One day, he appeared in my bedroom mirror. Good. Evil. I don't know what his true intentions are.

Enter Jackson, ghost hunting show host extraordinaire, and my ex, to save me from the big bad ghost.

From there…well…it's been a world wind of complications. My house burnt down. I'm being stalked by an ancient evil and gotten myself back into the world of being a ghost hunting psychic. Jackson dragged me, along with a few other psychics, to a ghost town wiped off the map called Death's Dance.

From there things went from bad to worse.

Death's Dance is Book One of the Deathly Encounters Series

Urban Fantasy from John F. Allen!
Meet Ivory Blaque!

Softcover: 978-1-937929-16-9
eBook: 978-1-937929-17-6

In The God Killers, the first book of The God Killers Legacy, former professional art thief Ivory Blaque is hired to procure a pair of antique pistols and gets much more than she bargained for when several attempts are made on her life.

Her client turns out to be a shadowy government agent who reveals that she is descended from a race of immortals, and that the pistols are linked to her unique heritage and the special psychic gifts she possesses. He uses the memory of her father to guilt her into working for him.

Ivory eventually gives in to his request, and in return, he presents her with her father's journal, which was written in an unbreakable code. Bishop believes that she is the only one capable of breaking the code and unlocking the plans of the vampire hierarchy. But when the city's top vampire is a sexy incubus with an attraction for her and she's assigned a hot new lycan enforcer to protect her, she finds herself caught between two sets of rock hard abs.

To regain her autonomy, clear her name, unlock the secrets of her past, and protect the lives of those closest to her, Ivory must play along with the forces trying to manipulate her. Ivory's life is rapidly spiraling out of control and headed for an explosive conclusion which she just might not survive.

Appalachian Gothic! Jason Sizemore's Irredeemable!
18 Tales of dark fantasy, science fiction, and horror

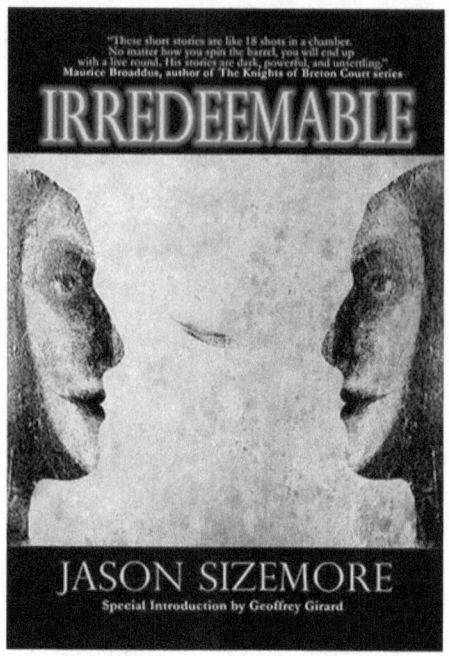

Softcover: 978-1-937929-59-6

eBook: 978-1-937929-68-8

Flowing like mists and shadows through the Appalachian Mountains come 18 tales from the mind of Jason Sizemore. Weaving together elements of southern gothic, science fiction, fantasy, horror, the supernatural, and much more, this diverse collection of short stories brings you an array of characters who must face accountability, responsibility, and, more ominously, retribution.

Whether it is Jack Taylor readying for a macabre, terrifying night in "The Sleeping Quartet," the Wayne brothers and mischief gone badly awry in "Pranks," the title character in "The Dead and Metty Crawford," or the church congregation and their welcoming of a special visitor in "Yellow Warblers," Irredeemable introduces you to a range of ordinary people who come face to face with extraordinary situations.

Whether the undead, aliens, ghosts, or killers of the yakuza, dangers of all kinds lurk within the darkness for those who dare tread upon its ground. Hop aboard and settle in, Irredeemable will take you on an unforgettable ride along a dark speculative fiction road.

www.ingramcontent.com/pod-product-compliance
Lightning Source LLC
Chambersburg PA
CBHW050505260626
47157CB00004B/1194